SUNDAY MONEY

SUNDAY MONEY

A NOVEL

MAGGIE HILL

SHE WRITES PRESS

Published 2024
Printed in the United States of America
Print ISBN: 978-1-64742-656-9
E-ISBN: 978-1-64742-657-6
Library of Congress Control Number: 2023918555

For information, address:
She Writes Press
1569 Solano Ave #546
Berkeley, CA 94707

Interior Design by Kiran Spees

She Writes Press is a division of SparkPoint Studio, LLC.

To all my heroes

Love is never any better than the lover.
—*Toni Morrison, The Bluest Eye*

May God protect me from gloomy saints.
—*St. Teresa of Avila*

AUGUST 1975

I'm sitting in the bleachers of Immaculata's gymnasium in Malvern, Pennsylvania. Took a Greyhound to get here before the semester begins, to try out for their famous basketball team. Basketball is no joke at Immaculata College. Last year, they played a televised game in Madison Square Garden. Televised! Girls' basketball! They won three consecutive national basketball championships from 1972 to 1974, just when everyone my age was giving up, trading years playing in the schoolyard for lipstick, making out, smoking pot. Not me, though. I'm the doofus who kept playing, even though I had a boyfriend, even though I was whispered to be a lezzie because I still laced up my Converse high-tops, showed up in the schoolyard, and practiced until sweat pasted the hair to my head.

When I signed in, one of the assistant coaches handed me a questionnaire: "Why do you want to try out for Immaculata's basketball team? What does basketball mean to you?"

With my knack for bullshitting teachers, I start to free-throw some poetic-sounding answers: the geometry of a well-set shot, the lazy spin of the ball swishing through the basket, the drilled cooperation of a team, et cetera, et cetera.

But the truth is, the answer to "What does basketball mean to me?" is deeper than what I am capable of explaining. My knees start bouncing, heart is beating, head feels ready to explode because I am somewhere I can't even believe I am, out of Brooklyn, out of my house, a little out of my mind.

I lay the paper aside, step out on the court to warm up.

The girls on the court know their stuff. They are easily laying up the ball, doing classic set shots, dribbling out and back. They're not showing off or acting like peacocks. They will bring it for the tryout. For now, they modestly size up the court and each other, take crisp and efficient shots, share the ball with the other players.

One girl sends me the ball, on a low bounce meant to feed into a three-dribble layup. I take it, feel the slight give of the floor, smell the just-washed varnish, my legs and feet fluid from years of playing. I restrain myself from doing a reverse layup—no showing off, no big movements. When it goes in, I just keep running to the top of the key, hopeful that the rebounder will send it to me again. She does. I take a quick foul shot, move in for the rebound or tip up, pass it to another waiting hopeful. Maybe six balls are going at once. Eyes are wide to know where everyone is, ready to react, to spring forward, backward, sideways.

Now I can breathe.

Basketball is civilized. There are rules, boundaries, time periods. It's about speed and accuracy. There's also the magic of it—seeing the whole court, concentrating, expecting the unexpected. It's eyes in the back of your head, legs crouching and flexing, dancing to the rhythm of a pounding leather ball.

And when there's nobody else on the court, only you and the basket, it's like a communion with an open net, ready to take your throw—the best kind of lonely. Being watched over, understood, *loved* even.

I sound like a nut. Just do your job.

FIRST QUARTER
1968

DRILL

My brother is going to teach me how to be good in basketball so I can join the local parish team and make friends in this new neighborhood. He is six feet one and a half inches; I am five feet nothing. He is seventeen; I am ten.

We go around the corner to Holy Child schoolyard. There are six half-courts, all taken. My brother says we'll practice passing while we wait for a court. He throws the ball, flicking both of his wrists. I can't catch it. I stagger when it lands on my chest. It's called a chest pass. He shows me how to take a knee-step back, catching the chest pass while I'm moving. Then we do bounce passes. I learn to gauge the throw so the force of the bounce sends the ball diagonally into my brother's outstretched hands.

Every boy in the schoolyard seems to know my brother. Last year, when he was a junior at Boys' High in Bedford-Stuyvesant, he was the New York City All-Star basketball team captain. Boys keep coming over, asking him if he wants to scrimmage. All of these boys are white. Everybody in Windsor Terrace is Irish or Italian, and they're all white, like us.

My brother is polite to these boys, but he doesn't hang around with them, or hang around here, or hang around with white boys. He hangs around in our old neighborhood in downtown Brooklyn.

A boy with red hair runs up to him, says our last name. "Joyce, we're starting a new game—you can be playmaker."

John says, "I'm playing with my sister right now."

The boy looks over at me, and I smile. He's looking right at me, but he doesn't see me. He turns back to John. "Why doesn't she play with girls?" He points his head at the corner of the schoolyard, where the girls' basketball team is practicing. Most of the girls are seventh and eighth graders. I would be the only fifth grader.

"She tried out for the team last week, but she didn't make it, so I'm teaching her some moves," John tells him.

We're still passing the ball back and forth, and now I try hitting my brother with a chest pass to his face. He catches the ball with no effort.

The boy opens his mouth, looks like he's going to say something nasty, but he walks away. Then he turns around. "When are you gonna be finished?" he asks.

Man, he really wants to play ball with my brother.

"We'll be finished after we play Around the World a couple of times," John tells him, still passing me the ball. The boy's face says he can't believe he's even having this conversation.

A court opens up, and we start playing Around the World. This is a game for concrete courts. Each square of concrete is one position. We start from directly underneath the basket. My brother shows me where to aim the ball against the backboard. If you get it in, you move to the second box. To go all the way around the world takes about twenty-four boxes.

I'm doing good, and I'm in the third box. My brother is going around for the second time, but he's only playing to break up the time in between my missed shots. Mostly, he's showing me how each box has a different angle for getting the ball in the basket.

The third box requires a swish shot. This means you have to aim the ball at the far rim of the basket with just enough height so it'll swish through the net, without touching the backboard. I'm having a hard time swishing it in. After ten or twelve tries, I still haven't sunk one, and my underarms and neck feel cramped. I'm losing my patience.

"Forget it. I stink."

"You do not stink. This is a hard shot—everybody has trouble with it at first. C'mon, this time arc the ball to just about here." He jumps up and points to the empty space a few inches from the basket.

"You told me to aim at the *far* rim!"

"Yeah, I know, but now I think that's too hard. You keep over-shooting the rim because you don't know how to control your power yet. That's okay; that's good, you can learn that later. You're strong—that's why this shot's so hard. It's closer to the basket, and you have to know how to ease the ball in. Try it like I say."

He gets an idea about how he'll jump up, and I'll aim the ball at his hand.

I concentrate on his hand. After a long time and a lot of jumping up on my brother's part, I finally get the ball in the basket.

"Two points for Little Miss!" he says.

I crack up. John sometimes uses a Southern accent and a high-pitched voice, calling my mother "Big Miss" and me "Little Miss." He got it from a play he read by Tennessee Williams.

We keep playing, sweating, shooting. The girls' basketball team practice is over, and I see them leaving, but I don't care. The school-yard is quieter; we go inside our heads. Time passes, and we are carried along with it. It's dusk. John includes me in his basketball loneness.

We move in and out of boxes. We play another round without talking. We concentrate, pivot and pass, start again. I would play Around the World all night if I could. John is right about the third box being hard because it's so close to the basket. The boxes farther out are much easier because they require more strength than skill. I'm strong.

All the way out at center court, John crouches with the ball. His legs are together as he dips low, then curls his body upward like an Olympic swimmer diving backward into a pool. He sends the ball arcing, arcing, high above the backboard, until it twirls downward, almost in slow motion, pulled by invisible energy toward the rim. John is still conducting the shot as he stands with his legs together, arms raised high and wide, two fingers on each hand straight, three each coiled, until the ball falls, without a sound, through the hoop.

KEY

On the way home, it's weakly light out. Almost dark. The neighborhood still feels new and strange. John walks with the basketball under his arm, no bouncing or twirling. We moved here at the end of summer, right around when school started. Holy Child is the parish, and the schoolyard is where everyone goes. Everyone plays basketball, every day, morning until night. I'm tired. I start thinking about whether it's a drinking night or not. My mother is not an everyday drunk. She drinks in the kitchen by herself. Beer. Rheingold. Six cans. If she drank last night, then she won't be drinking tonight. All I have to remember is what she did last night. At least John will be home tonight. That makes it easier.

Our apartment is on the third floor over a pizza shop on the avenue, right down the block from the church and around the corner from the schoolyard. We trot up the two flights in the dark hallway and open the door. It's always unlocked. The window on the door is frosted with a raised design on it, like bumps, so you can't see anyone inside or outside. It doesn't look like the door to an apartment. Inside, there's a long hallway in front of you, and to the left, a door that opens into two bedrooms. When you walk down the long hallway, the bathroom is on the left and the little cubby room with the TV is right after it. Then comes the living room, where my oldest brother, Martin, sleeps. Through the archway from the living room is the kitchen. My mother is sitting at the kitchen table, lifting a small glass of Rheingold to her lips.

"I needed Robert to go to the store, so dinner won't be ready for a little while," she says.

"Great—when did he go?" John asks.

"He just came home. I sent him right out," she says.

"What are we having?" I ask.

"Whatever I make," she says.

"That's always true," I say. "But what are you making tonight?"

"I'm making dinner tonight, miss. Now wash up and get yourself ready."

I'm about to ask her why she has to be so grouchy, when John pulls out his Suave Guy act. He starts talking in a British accent and pretends he's at a big social event wearing a tuxedo. "I say, old girl, looking forward to dining at Joyce Haute Cuisine tonight. Shall we have a dance while the maids and butlers prepare our feast?" He pulls her out of the chair, whisks her around the kitchen in a little dance, and bows as he returns her to her chair. Now the grouch is laughing, and her whole mood is changed. Suave Guy works every time.

"Stop this nonsense," she says, laughing. "I'm making chicken fricassee, and you'll be dining by seven o'clock. So cheerio, young man. The dinner bell will ring presently."

John goes to the bathroom. I pick up my book bag in the cubby room even though I already did my homework. When I come home from school, I usually sit down and finish it up as fast as I can. I don't like having to do it later, because you don't know whether it's going to be quiet or loud in the house. It depends on the drinking.

John comes back out as Bobby comes in with a bag of groceries. Bobby's thirteen, and he was able to get into Holy Child because they had room in the boys' school. I'm still going to St. A's because the girls' school is full. My mother came with me on the bus on the first day of school, just to take the ride. That was a nervous trip for her. It's like she's thinking of all the things that can go wrong, even when nothing is going wrong.

"I'm going to meet up with Julius. We'll grab a slice later," John says. He's wearing his new black leather jacket he said he got from Julius's uncle. My mother calls John black Irish, like her, because he's got dark hair and dark brown eyes. His hair is wet now, slicked back, and his tannish face is shiny from just being washed. Even I know he's handsome.

"What do you mean? It's a school night. What time will you be home?" my mother says. She is practically stuttering.

John calls out from the hallway as he walks toward the door, "I'll be home by eleven, Big Miss. See you later." He stops by the cubby archway, says to me, "Homework done? Any tests tomorrow?"

I shake my head at him, yes and no, give him a thumbs-up. He gives me one back and keeps walking. He always asks me about my books, my homework, my school, my friends. It's almost like he's really interested in what I'm doing.

But he's on his second high school already. First he went to Xavier in Manhattan on a scholarship, but he didn't do his work, and he didn't like their basketball team. At Boys' High, after the all-star game last year, he started getting in trouble for playing hooky. My mother had to go up to see the principal.

John can be a real jerk, even if he is my favorite person in the whole family. He is usually so cool. He walks with a beat. Like, one leg stretches out in front of him, and the other jerks at the knee to catch up to it. When the other leg is jerking, his chin points out in the direction that he's walking. Then he pulls his head back in with his neck. He walks better than some people dance.

My mother goes back to the kitchen, where Bobby is taking out the onions and rice from the bag. I come in to help. "Just leave me be in here," she says, taking another beer out of the fridge. I peek in to count how many are gone. That's the third—not good.

Bobby goes to his bedroom. I am in the cubby room, with the TV news on low, looking at images of American soldiers in Vietnam. My mother is in the kitchen, preparing for the war she will have after the next couple of beers.

I wish my father was home. Sometimes he will say to my mother, "Kate, stop it," with his low, gravelly voice, and she just . . . stops. My father is a cabdriver, and he works nights. He leaves at three thirty in the afternoon, when we're coming home from school. Sometimes Bobby and I pass him on the stairs, and we say hi. He's been driving a cab around New York City for more than twenty-five years. He started with IOTA Cab Company after he got out of the army. He was in Guadalcanal when he was seventeen. That's all we know. It's hard to picture.

My father fixes everything in the house with black masking tape. He really thinks that stuff is great. Like, between the kitchen and the living room there's a strip of black masking tape keeping the split-off ends of the linoleum down. And the end table has four balls of black masking tape around each leg. Each leg isn't broken, but when he fixed the broken one, he wrapped all four legs to keep the table even.

My father works seven days a week, hardly ever taking a day off. When he does, he sleeps all day and gets up at the same time as when he leaves for work. I never think of him as a cabdriver like the way cabdrivers look on TV. On TV, they're always tough, cigar-smoking wise guys who know everything and wear caps on their heads. My father is a sad-looking, slow-walking, bent-over old man.

Except when he's ossified. My mother always says he's ossified when she means he's drunk. She's usually drunk too. Drunk happens a lot in our house.

Sometimes when my mother is drinking beer, she'll ask John to do Suave Guy for her. He won't, though. He only does Suave Guy when he feels like it.

I can smell the chicken; we'll eat soon. It's almost six thirty. Maybe there will be a pregame show on the Knicks if they have a game tonight. I love watching the Knicks. Sometimes John will watch a game with me, and even Bobby. John talks about Walt Frazier, Dave DeBusschere, and Earl "the Pearl" Monroe like he knows them. My secret favorite is Bill Bradley, but that's because he's not so much like a star. He's just a solid player, always good, reliable. I really like Willis Reed, too, but he's crazy tall. I like the way Bill Bradley dribbles the ball—he always looks like he's on his way somewhere, and he really wants to go there. Walt Frazier looks like he's thinking about something, and Earl Monroe always looks like he's trying to fake someone out, even when nobody is guarding him. When Phil Jackson dribbles, I think he's going to fall down because his arms swing so far away from his body.

"Come on out here now and have your supper," my mother calls. Not one second later, she runs into the cubby and starts yelling. "Turn that TV off—what are you looking at? Don't you dare watch this disgusting news about those poor boys over in that hellhole!"

"What do you mean?" I yell back. "I'm just changing channels waiting for dinner!"

"Don't you dare watch this garbage!" she screams. She switches off the TV like she is punching it in the face. Bobby has come out from the bedroom. He's shaking his head at me not to say any more, but I'm not going to let her yell at me for no reason. It isn't fair.

"Stop screaming at me! I'm not doing anything!" I yell.

"Get in that kitchen and eat your dinner, miss. And don't be taking that tone with me," she says. She begins her muttering.

The food is food, and we eat fast. My mother doesn't eat; she sits at her place at the table, looking off somewhere she alone can see. Bobby is eating just so he can go back into his room and listen to his Beatles album. He's wearing his blank face, but I know he's holding his breath because this is just the beginning of the night's yelling. I feel so mad, I could spit right on the kitchen floor.

My mother's friend, Mae Doyle, gave Bobby *Revolver* for Christmas last year. He knows every word of every song. I don't understand it. They used to be good, the Beatles, but "Yellow Submarine"? It's dumb. We definitely don't all live in a yellow submarine. For Bobby, it's like the song lyrics are the answer to every question he never asked.

I have questions too. They are inside me, not being asked. They're brewing, like my father's percolator coffee pot that he uses every afternoon before he leaves for work. Like, I wonder why I don't feel God after I receive communion on Sunday. And I wonder why I always have to be good, when I feel like saying, "Just shut up" to my mother, to Sister Charles, and to some of the stupid people I see every day. Why do I have to be nice?

I only just started playing basketball, and I don't know what I'm doing yet. But I know that I can slam that ball, dribble hard, bounce it out, and learn. I am getting on that girls' team my next tryout. Just wait and see.

ONE=ON=ONE

"**N**obody wants to be friends," I say as I walk into the kitchen where my mother and oldest brother, Martin, are talking. He lives here, but he sleeps on the high-rise bed in the living room. He's always walking in and out, going to or coming from work, back from the bar or going out to the bar. He's twenty-two. He seems *older*, like a construction worker bar guy. We actually have the same birth date, twelve years apart, so we have something in common. There's a 1-in-365 chance of that, according to *Encyclopedia Britannica*.

"Did you ask one of the girls to play with you?" my mother says.

I've just been standing around since three thirty watching the girls' team do defense practice. When they were almost finished, I left and came back home.

"They were practicing. They can't play with me when they're practicing!"

"I know that," she says, being nice because she knows I'm yelling at her because I just am. "But when they're finished, you can play, can't you?"

"They don't want to play with me. They just want to play with each other. I don't care!"

"So make them want to play with you. Go back there and smile that grand smile of yours, and ask them if you can play too." She's smiling her grand smile at me.

Martin opens the kitchen window and sticks his head out. From the fire escape, we can see the schoolyard. He says, "There's three girls playing now. Run over and see if you can get in on a pickup game."

"That's easy for you to say."

Martin used to be a great guard before he quit school. He was like the dependable player who helps the real stars, like John, get clear for the shot. He doesn't play anymore; he just works and goes to the bar. Now that I think about it, why is he in the kitchen with my mother this afternoon?

"What are you doing home?" I say.

"Don't I live here?"

"You know what I mean. How come you're home?"

He laughs. "How come *you're* home? Why aren't you in the schoolyard playing with kids your own age? Oh yeah, that's right. Nobody wants to *plaaaay* with you."

"That's enough," my mother says. "Now go play while you have the chance. We're eating at six, beef stew, so hurry up."

I wait a few seconds. It doesn't feel like anything's wrong here; maybe they're just having a conversation. If anything was wrong, they wouldn't be so calm and interested in who's playing with me. I go back out, determined to make friends in the schoolyard.

Kelly Shea has red hair, like a sunburn. It sits on top of her six-foot body like it's getting ready to peel. She is the star of the girls' basketball team, and she's playing a one-on-one game with her cousin Shirley Mackie. I'm standing with my back against the fence, watching them.

They're both breathing hard, but Kelly is louder. She has total concentration on the ball, the basket, both of their feet. Shirley's eyes look fierce, and she has an evil smirk as she bumps up against Kelly, trying to steal. I know this has something to do with psyching Kelly out, trying to get her on the run and scared. Kelly does not look directly at Shirley, not even once. She is playing to the basket, checking Shirley's position only by where her feet go. But Shirley is looking directly at Kelly's face as she moves her hands up, down, out toward the ball. It's like she's taunting Kelly, like she's saying, "You're too scared to face me." I know they're friends, because they are always together, but this game is not friendly.

Kelly fakes left and turns right for the shot, brushing up against Shirley's shoulder with her shooting arm. She sinks it.

"You walked, you walked!" Shirley says, right in Kelly's face as she is taking the ball out.

Kelly's cheeks turn redder, but she takes the ball out past the foul line and rushes in for another basket. She sinks it. As she starts to take the ball out again, Shirley slaps it away from her and scores an easy layup. Now it's Shirley's turn to control the game.

Kelly stands a whole arm's length away from Shirley with her hands waving horizontally, then vertically, as if she were a new cheer-leader who can't keep up with the chant. She's blocking the shot, and Shirley hasn't taken the shot yet. It's not a strong move; she should be blocking Shirley. The smirk on Shirley's face is so ugly, I'm getting mad at it just standing here by the fence.

Shirley fakes, shoots, scores, takes it out, then seems to stroll to the basket for another shot. Kelly doesn't even try to catch up. Now Shirley is crouching, holding the ball, like she has all the time in the world to set up her shot. Kelly gives her the time. I have to shut my lips together so I won't yell out, "Grab the ball, Kelly!" Meanwhile, Shirley stands at the foul line, completely uncovered, to take the shot. She misses. Kelly grabs the rebound and laughs out loud on the way to take it out. It's the kind of laugh you can't hold in, a justice kind of laugh. I'm smiling inside.

Shirley's not even pretending to be cool. She is all over Kelly, shadowing her. "Keep laughing, Shea," she says. "Don't move so fast, or you might trip over your feet."

My brother Bobby knows a lot about the people in the schoolyard because he goes to school here. He's in the same grade as Kelly and Shirley. One night at supper, Bobby told us all about how Kelly beats Shirley at basketball every day, and how Shirley hates her guts. He told us that Shirley backstabs Kelly every chance she gets – making fun of her hair, her height, even her feet—right to her face!—but Kelly never says anything back. She just takes it. "Girls," Bobby said. "They're so stupid."

Martin laughed out loud, John shook his head, and my mother said some prayerish thing, like "May the angels." I was creeped out, picturing having a friend who hates me. Why would Kelly stay friends with her? To play basketball? Because she feels bad about herself, too, and Shirley knows it? Picturing Kelly, I know she has enough going against her, what with her size and her not-good-looking face. She didn't need pity. She needed to stick up for herself.

I force myself to look straight at Shirley's face, practicing not being afraid of her.

Shirley shouldn't have made out-loud fun of Kelly's feet, because Kelly got her back by running away with the game. Before, Kelly must have just been playing to practice. Now she's stomping her all over the court.

A smaller-sized Shirley runs into the schoolyard, saying, "Mommy says to tell you to let me play, Shirley!"

Shirley looks over at her it-has-to-be sister like she was a fly that just droned by. "Yeah, all right. We're finished here."

It's like instead of losing, she just decided the game was over. Kelly starts throwing the ball in the basket, and whoever gets the rebound shoots. Shirley's sister runs around after the ball and takes shots. None of the shots are any good, I'm happy to see. She's definitely the same age as me.

All of a sudden, Kelly looks right at me. "You wanna play?" The ends of her hair are pointed with sweat, and she has some spit in the corner of her mouth.

I say, "Yeah, all right," like I wasn't standing there for the last half hour.

Kelly tells Shirley it'll be Shirley and Lily against me and her. "What's your name?" she asks.

"Claire."

We take the ball out first, which means I throw the ball to Kelly, and she basically plays one-on-one with Shirley again. I'm glad, because I stink anyway. My only worry is that Kelly will try to pass the ball back to me. So I run around getting out of Lily's way, who is guarding me like crazy, even though I don't have the ball. Kelly is scoring, scoring, scoring. I am great at passing the ball to her when I take it out.

Then Shirley slaps it out of Kelly's hands and goes in for a layup. I do not know where I get this idea. I just do it—I don't think. As Shirley starts toward the basket, I lose Lily and come behind Shirley. I run one step in front of her, then turn around and knock the ball, like John showed me, out from her dribbling hand. I knock it with too much might, though, and it slams away from both of us and goes out of bounds. Like, far out of bounds. They all look at me. "That was out on me," I say, like I do this every day. Nobody says anything, nobody smiles, nobody gets mad, nobody does anything except play after I retrieve the ball from the next court. It's like I'm the only witness to this miracle of defense I just performed.

We play for another twenty minutes or so, and I don't do anything except pass the ball to Kelly when we take it out, run away from Lily, and hold a secret thrill that I stole the ball from the second-best player on the girls' basketball team—which I didn't make when I tried out for it two months ago.

When we finish the game, the three of them start out of the schoolyard before me. I'm walking behind them. Kelly turns around at the gate and says, "See you tomorrow, Claire." I couldn't wait to tell everybody at home.

* *

Of course, John isn't home when I get there. Martin is gone. Bobby is somewhere but not there. My mother is in the kitchen reading a library book, *The Confessions of Nat Turner*, which must be pretty good, because she doesn't hear me come in.

"Hi. Where'd Martin go?" I ask.

She looks up from her glasses, adjusting to this world from the world of the book. "He's out with friends, I think. You look all sweaty. Did you play basketball?"

"Yeah, I played with some girls in the schoolyard." I'm acting all casual, like I have played with these girls every day since we moved here.

"Good! Let's get dinner started," she says, closing the book, taking off her glasses, and wrapping an apron around her waist. "Why don't you wash up, like a good girl, and I'll have your dinner soon. Bobby is at a basketball game at Bishops, so he won't be home for a while. Is there something good on television you want to watch? I wouldn't mind a movie. See what's on."

"Are you eating dinner too?"

"Yes, I'll eat with you." She's pulling out a box of linguini and a can of Progresso clam sauce—seriously, one of my favorites.

I do a quick cleanup in the bathroom and check my books, though it's Friday, so I don't really have to. School is so easy. I honestly wish it was harder, so I'd have to work for all these stupid 90s, like my friend Maureen.

I look up the movies in the *TV Guide* and come up with *Three Faces of Eve*. Sounds like something my mother would like. Turns out, she's more excited than I am about it. We finish up our plates, her telling me that she might work for the election board in a couple of weeks. "Money for Christmas," she says. Sounds good to me.

The movie is about a woman who is split up into three people.

Like, she turns into a bad woman, then an intelligent woman. She starts out being a scared, good woman.

"Oh, that Eve Black!" my mother says. "She's a *divil*."

I say, "Poor Eve White. She's going crazy!"

During the commercial, we pick our favorites for who will end up being the real Eve in the end. I bet on Eve White, figuring everyone wants her to be quiet and good instead of wild and bad, or not to know who you are at all, like the third personality.

My mother is determined it has to be Jane, Eve's third personality. She lights a cigarette, saying, "Eve White's weak. She'll never make it."

"But she's so good. What do you mean she's weak?"

She lets out a big stream of smoke. "Yes, I know Eve White is good, but she can't take anything. She's afraid all the time. That's why that other devil came out, to show her that she can do anything she damn well pleases. But she goes too far! So that's why Jane came out—she's the smart one. She'll win. You watch and see."

When the movie ends, Jane wins. I feel proud of my mother for being right. I tell her so.

"Of course I was right," she says. "I saw that movie when it first came out."

"What? How come you acted like you never saw it before?" I walk behind her as she goes to the bathroom, the kitchen, and back to the living room.

She says, "Because then I wouldn't've enjoyed it. And you would have kept asking me what was going to happen next."

I'm insulted. "No, I wouldn't've. You could have told me. No wonder you picked Jane. I bet you didn't pick Jane the first time you saw it. Did you? Who did you pick the first time you saw it?"

"Oh, stop this nonsense. I don't remember picking any one of them. I just watched the movie. What are you so mad about?"

"Because you didn't tell me. Because you act crazy sometimes too." There—said it.

We are back in the living room, and my mother sits down in an armchair. She says, "You think you're so smart, don't you, miss? You think I'm going to get mad because you say I act crazy sometimes? Well, I've got news for you. I'm even crazier than you think."

"What do you mean? You're not crazy."

"You're so smart, but you don't know what I mean. Yes, I am crazy. But I'm not talking about running around the streets like that Eve Black. I'm talking about how in my mind I feel crazy. Think about it."

That stops me from talking. I flip around in my head, trying to come up with another answer for her. Does she know she's only crazy when she drinks? Is she crazier than I thought? What is happening in her head? Thinking about what she said leaves me not knowing if what I think is true or right. She tells riddles like that a lot. I always fall for them.

Just before I go to bed, I get afraid that maybe it isn't all over for "Jane." Maybe Eve White and Eve Black will come back every once in a while to haunt her. I ask my mother if this is possible. She says that anything is possible, but could we talk about it in the morning? She's exhausted. It's only nine thirty.

Then John comes home. His black leather jacket is hanging on him like he doesn't have any shoulders, rounding down from his neck into two long arms. He smells like bacon grease. Just as he walks in, he turns around to walk out. My mother asks him where he's going, what he's doing, why he's leaving. He can't answer her and keeps shaking his head back and forth, up and down, as if he's making sense. He tries to go around her, like he's going to go out. But he just came home. It doesn't make sense.

My mother is blocking the doorway so he won't go out. She's standing very straight and tall, her arms spread out on the door-jambs. Her cigarette ash is so low it looks like it will burn her hand. I reach out to flick the ash.

"Get in the front room and get in bed," she says, excited. "Now I don't know what's wrong with you—are you drunk?—but you're not going out of this house like that. Go on, now. Go on."

"I'm not drunk. Okay, I'm a little drunk. I had a few beers. It's Friday night! Okay, Ma? C'mon, be a good miss and let me go, okay?"

He's smiling, but it's a mushy smile, almost like he's drunk. But he isn't. He's something else. His nose is runny, he keeps pulling on his chin, and his eyes seems like they can't focus.

"Well, never mind. You're going to eat something and have a cup of coffee before you're ever getting out of this house tonight, so take that coat off and turn around like a good boy and get into the kitchen."

He's so nice to her. He stares at her for a minute, then chuckles somebody else's laugh and turns around. It takes him the whole length of the hallway to get his jacket off. He is moving in slow motion. I'm walking behind him, worrying that he is going to fall. My mother is walking backward in front of him, as if she's a magnet and he has to obey her force field.

"Big Miss," he says, "I'm going to be late."

"That's the breaks," she says, trying to sound cool.

I feel like pushing him, not just to hurry him up. He is acting like a jerk.

My mother wants to feed him because food in the stomach sobers people up. She knows something is more wrong than that, though. He sits in the kitchen by the wall, looking at nothing, eyes half open. My mother keeps looking at him as she puts a piece of flank steak in the frying pan. She moves back and forth from the stove to the middle of the table, like she thinks he is going to fall. I am behind him, standing in the archway between the kitchen and the living room. His eyes are opening, closing, like a blink that got stuck, and he has a wrong-looking smile on his lips. His head nods, then snaps up, like he just fell asleep on the train and thinks he missed his stop. He turns toward me, says, "Hey, Little Miss, do we have any soda?"

I'm looking him hard in the eyes, mad.

My mother says, "No, no, now. I'm making coffee. Just one more minute, and it'll be ready." She flips her eyes toward me. "Do we have milk? Check the fridge. Maybe you can go get a quart of milk. Take money from my bag, and go to the store. Get yourself a snack. Get going."

Five minutes ago, we were heading to bed. Now she is trying to fake me out and get rid of me. I plead with my eyes for her to let me stay and help. I am afraid to say anything out loud. She knows it. She shakes her head at me, tells me again to get going because we need the milk for the coffee. She looks so nervous, when she should be mad at him. I don't think she knows what to do, and until she figures it out, she doesn't want any witnesses.

Keeping John home is the answer, my mother must think. He's been arrested two times already—once for joyriding, once for possession of drugs. If looks alone can get you arrested, he qualifies. This John in the kitchen looks like those guys on the parkside who blow their noses and drink white cartons of beer from Farrell's Bar & Grill. I feel a wind starting in my chest, like I'm in the first car of the Cyclone as it climbs up the first hill. Before it gets to the top, I go lie down on my bed. Forget the stupid milk.

I recite the Memorare, which is a prayer my mother says when she goes to novenas. A couple of years ago, she stopped drinking for Lent and went to novenas every single night for forty days. It was awful. I had to go with her. But I learned the Memorare because it has phrases like poetry, which are rhythmic, sometimes hard to pronounce. It clears my mind. Once I get past the first group of phrases—"Remember, O most precious Virgin Mary, that ever was it known, that anyone who fled to thy protection, implored thy help, or sought thy intercession, was left unaided"—I almost feel like I'm dribbling a basketball, bounce, bounce, and the rest of everything stops.

FOUL

We moved here about six months after John was arrested, when the court case was finished. But we didn't move because of John; we moved because of Bobby. Or really because of the priests at St. A's, for suspending Bobby from the basketball team for fighting with one of his teammates in seventh grade. They told my mother he was one step away from being a "juvenile delinquent." Bobby said the kid fouled him behind the ref's back, but they didn't believe him. My mother was fit to be tied. After she had her beers in the kitchen, she yelled about how the priests were bastards who were too quick to sacrifice her sons. She said if we were the Connellys, they would have bent over backward to make sure their precious son didn't even get his hair mussed. The Connellys live in a brownstone on First Street, and my mother resents them. She says bad things about them, using words I'm not supposed to say. I think she knows Mrs. Connelly from a long time ago. I feel bad for the Connellys because their daughter, who is in my class, has such a hard time with reading and math. Sister Charles is always helping her, trying to make her understand, but Julia always ends up crying. Crying in the fourth grade is bad enough, but fifth grade is way too old. She should know that. Nobody in my house would ever put up with that. Their son, Henry, was on Bobby's basketball team, and if Bobby says the kid fouled him, then he did. Bobby doesn't lie. He hits.

So we moved in the middle of fourth grade for me, middle of seventh for Bobby. As I've said, they had room in Holy Child for Bobby, but the girls' school was full. I have a bus pass and take two buses to school in the morning. I love it. Getting to school is like a challenge—can I run fast enough to make the Seventh Avenue bus before it pulls away? Plus, there's no kids on either of these buses. It's mostly adults on their way to work downtown, so I'm invisible to them. I get to look at them without interruptions.

My bus stop is at the beginning of the bus route, so I get the same seat every day—all the way in the back, last seat on the right. This way I can get a look at people waiting for the bus before they get on. Two ladies always stand out.

One lady gets on near Eighth Avenue and Fifteenth Street. She sits in the front first seat, near the entrance. She says hello to the bus driver like she's a visiting bus company executive. The bus driver welcomes her on his bus. This lady is white, and she wears a starched, lean trench coat, belted tight; her nude stockings go perfectly with her brand-new-looking, tan, sensible heels. She pivots toward her seat, sitting down straight, legs crossed, one hand on the seat pole. She wears glasses, but not in a doofy way. It's like they even add to her look. She's not beautiful or anything like that. She just has this organized, traveling look about her. The bus driver nods officially at her, friendly, every day. She rides the bus for only a few stops. I always figure she's a teacher or maybe a college professor. She has a look like she's in the world.

When I transfer to the Seventh Avenue bus, I never know where I'm going to sit, or if I'm getting a seat. My favorite lady on this bus gets on before I get off. She is what you would call sexy. She is dark, dark brown, tall, and always wears matching-color high heels to what-ever color dress or suit she's wearing. She has brown, orange-ish hair, which sounds clownish but is really beautiful. It waves all around her head, coming to just below her ears, which have gold hoop earrings dropping down. Her suits are nubby, like mohair, and so colorful with those matching heels. Sometimes they're bright orange or deep green. She walks down the whole aisle of the bus, sticking out in front and in back, her head practically bouncing off the ceiling. She doesn't make eye contact with anyone, because she looks like she has something on her mind, like she is already where she is going or they're waiting for her to arrive, or maybe she's wondering if she turned off the iron in her house before she left. If she notices the bug eyes on the men, she'd have to either laugh or be embarrassed. I always imagine she's going downtown to one of the big stores; maybe she is the manager. I look for her when my mother takes me to A&S to shop, but I never see her there. I never see her anywhere except the bus.

Between those two ladies is some kind of future me, I hope. I definitely want to be big enough to fill up a whole bus aisle with turning heads, and I want to be crisp and official to make even the bus driver welcome me aboard like I matter.

On the way home from school, I start to figure out if it's a drinking night—after I transfer to the Smith Street bus, usually. By the time I reach the crucifix on Holy Child, I already have my plan.

If it's a regular night, I'll come home and change my uniform, maybe grab a snack, stare at my mother a little bit in the kitchen so she knows I didn't forget last night. Then I'll run over to the schoolyard to practice. First, does she need anything from the store?

If it's a drinking night, I'll change my uniform, do my homework really fast—I mean like in ten or fifteen minutes, no matter how much I have—and avoid her eyes when I tell her I'm going out, see her at six. Does she need anything from the store?

Sounds the same, but it's different, believe me.

On drinking nights, six comes fast. Even if I wanted to stay out later, everybody goes home by then except a few boys in the schoolyard. When I go up the stairs to my house, I basically get myself prepared, organizing the time until bedtime. All the thinking goes on outside the door, because once I get inside, there's just being there.

KINGS

The girls' Catholic Youth Organization basketball team is excellent. Their coaches are older girls who are almost women. They take themselves seriously. Not like at St. A's, where the basketball team is intramural and nobody cares whether the girls can play or not. At St. A's, they're just basically getting fresh air and exercise. Here, it's different. These girls are really playing ball! They're sweating, running, fouling. Watching them, I know this is what I'm going to do in sixth grade. I'm going to be on that team. I'm going to be as good as anyone, and maybe a little better than the weakest players. I watch them practice. I follow the shot placements, the dribbling speeds, the different defenses. When the team leaves the schoolyard, I pick up one of the balls and practice. Start with a few set shots, play Around the World, dribble down and back court, try some layups, even a hook shot or two. Nobody is in the schoolyard near six, so it's just me and the ball. Usually when the janitor comes at six thirty, I leave the ball and go home. Until then, I'm playing man-on-man defense, against myself.

"Want to play Kings?" A shortish girl who looks my age is standing outside the boundary line of the court.

"Sure," I say. I bounce her the ball and she scoops it up, starting to dribble. She moves in toward the basket, shoots, and it's a good shot, but it doesn't go in. I grab the rebound and send it back to her. She looks surprised, but she dribbles again, sets up the shot. This time, it goes in.

"Want to start?" she asks. "Hey, my friend Diane might be coming out too. She does homework until now, but she'll be finished soon. Can she play?"

"Yes, sure," I say. Now I'm dribbling, left to right, right to left, actually trying to look better than I am. I'm not fooling her.

"I didn't make the team, either," she says. "I'm Tina."

"Claire. How did you know I didn't make the team?"

"Because it was you, me, and Diane who didn't make it. What are you in, fifth?"

"Yeah, you?" I'm doing easy layups and not looking at her. I'm half-embarrassed, half-mad that she is talking about me not making the team. I don't care if she didn't make it, but I feel weird that she knows my business.

"Yes. Your brother goes here. Why don't you?" Tina asks.

"No room," I say.

"Right," she says. She tries to get me to throw her the ball by putting her hands out, but I'm too busy ignoring her eyes.

Another girl, a little older, runs toward us. She is about my height, and she looks Italian because her skin is tan, and her hair and eyes are brown. Definitely not black Irish. Tina is definitely Italian because she has dark hair, flipped up, a headband, and dark eyes.

"Hi, I'm Diane," says the light brown girl. She has a flip too and a headband. I suddenly am aware of what I look like. I'm wearing Bobby's old black high-top Converse sneakers, and I have a bobby pin keeping back my bangs that my mother cuts, and they're always crooked.

"Hey," I say.

"What are we playing? Kings?" Diane asks.

"Not yet," Tina says, looking at me. "Want to start?"

"Oh, sure." I stand at the foul line and try to make the shot. It misses, but Tina has it, and she runs to a spot where nobody is so she can shoot. Diane stands underneath the basket, crouching, ready to catch it. Kings is a game where whoever catches the ball, if it doesn't go in the basket, has to shoot from where they catch it. If the ball goes in, the catcher has to catch it with one hand. It's a real run-around-a-lot type of game, and a lot more fun with three people than with two. Tina is a fast breaker, quick shooter, quick dribbler. Diane is steady, sets up her shot, pounces on the ball rather than chasing it. I'm a little bit of both. Tina is winning. She has G, and there's only one letter left. She catches my missed shot, lays it up, makes it. She wins.

"Want to play Around the World?" I ask.

Diane shakes her head. "I have to be home by six thirty. I was lucky to get out of the house for this long. Finals all next week."

Tina asks me, "Are you taking finals at your school?"

"We have the same academic schedule," I say. "Are you guys going to try out for the team again?"

"Of course," says Tina. "They'll have tryouts right after the end of school, so we can practice all summer. You're trying out, right?"

"Definitely," I say.

"You'll definitely make it," Tina says. "You're good."

I am truly happy she said that and now believe she is the nicest person in the world. "You too," I say. "And you too, Diane."

Diane shakes her head, not so sure. "I'm going into eighth grade, so they have their starters already. I'm probably not going to make it."

"What are you talking about?" says Tina. "We'll practice every day until tryouts, then we'll practice all summer. You'll be here every day, right? Will you, Claire?"

"I will be here every day," I promise. But there's a part of me that thinks Diane might be right. She's going into eighth grade? Tina and I are only going into sixth. We can be really good by eighth grade. Diane is solid and strong, but she doesn't handle the ball well, and she takes a long time to shoot.

We start walking out of the schoolyard. Diane says, "Your brother is really cute."

I think she means John, so I say, "He's a senior in high school."

"No, I mean the one who goes here, the one in eighth grade," she says.

Tina starts laughing. "His name is Bobby, and you know it, Diane," she says. To me, she says, "All the girls have a crush on him."

I am disgusted by this. Bobby? What is wrong with these girls? I don't say anything, but they see my face, and Diane looks concerned, but Tina laughs.

"Oh, come on, it doesn't mean anything," she says. "So big deal, some of the girls think he's cute. So what? Let's play basketball tomorrow, okay? What time will you be here?"

"I don't care who anybody likes or doesn't like," I say. "I just think it's moronic." Diane looks hurt, so I say, "Diane, do you have homework until six tomorrow? Can you come earlier?"

"I'll try to get out as soon as I can," she says. She is sweet and kind of a worried type of girl.

We walk around the corner from the schoolyard. They live next door to each other on the block with the porches and houses where only one family lives. I say goodbye to them. This is going to be good. Practice every day, and even figure out the whole summer playing while I'm at it.

I'm wondering how these girls were never in the schoolyard before. They must have seen me playing by myself and decided to come over and play. How long did they think about it? Did they see me play with Kelly Shea a couple of months ago? That was the only time I played with her, but I've seen her since. She doesn't actually say hello to me, but she kind of nods like she knows I'm there. The other one, Shirley, walks by me as if I was not even worth moving her eyes in my direction. I vow never to be like that when I'm in eighth grade and as good as they are. I'm going to be nice to the young girls and help them learn how to play. Unless they're moronic like Shirley's sister, Lily.

By the time I'm back at the door to our apartment, I haven't even thought of anything but my own thoughts. I love basketball.

Bobby's in his room, so I knock on the wall outside the curtain. He's listening to the Rolling Stones, another favorite.

"What?" he says.

"You're a big star with the girls at Holy Child," I say, smug.

"What are you talking about?"

I try to see him the way Tina and Diane see him, but this just makes me laugh. I snort, "'Oh, your brother's so cute.'"

Bobby is off the bed and in my face before I have time to react. He smashes me against the wall, then punches me in the stomach. "Shut up, or next time I'll smack you in the face," he whispers fiercely.

I am stunned and can't catch my breath. I feel fear and rage all the way down to my sneakers. I push him back, but he grabs my hair and pulls it down almost to the ground. It feels like he's ripping it out. I scream out loud.

My mother yells from down the hallway, "What's going on in there? Claire?"

I try to scream to her, but Bobby puts his hand over my mouth with such force that I can't breathe. I try to bite his hand, but my mouth can't move. Bobby's face is in my face, and he tells me to shut up. I nod, my eyes swearing I won't say anything.

I forgot. Bobby looks like he's mild and nice, but he is a maniac underneath. He's scary. He's been twisting my arms, punching me around, even choking me one time, since forever. It's always sneaky, and it's always alone. He doesn't just say he's going to smack you in the face—he does it. I run out of the room.

"Don't come in here again," he yells after me.

I run to my mother in the kitchen. "Bobby just punched me in the stomach and almost killed me." I am crying. My stomach is cramping. My throat is sore. Worse than anything, I'm so insulted that somebody can punch me around just like that.

My mother looks at my face, touches my shoulder, walks to Bobby's bedroom. I'm sitting in the kitchen chair by the wall, trying not to wail out loud, wanting to, holding a napkin to my running nose. Getting hit feels like the flu, which I had once—stiffness, pain, not being able to swallow, and a big headache on my whole face.

I hate Bobby. He is mental, and nobody knows it but me. We are all just better off if he is left alone, listening to his music. I hear murmuring from the other side of the hall but not anybody getting in big trouble. What he did is bad but is not big trouble for some reason. My mother wants him to logically know he can't do this, like last time, but other than her stern talk, nothing will happen to him. Nothing happened last time, either.

It's quiet in the kitchen. A sleepy feeling comes over me. I blow my nose. The refrigerator's low motor sounds like sweet noise. The yellow-and-white-checkered curtain around the bottom of the sink seems friendly and calm. Even the wooden kitchen chair feels warm. The voices down the hall are quiet; nobody screams.

TIME IN

I'm worried about John. What's happening to him? All of a sudden, like the moment of suspension in a jump shot, he quits school, stops playing basketball, gets a job on Wall Street, comes home to give my mother money, goes back out. Almost like Martin, and even my father, he's like a guest in the house, or a boarder. Why won't anyone ask him what's what? Does anyone care that he's a different person? He starts to come into the house looking like one of those messed-up guys on the parkside, the guys who hang out, smoke cigarettes, have white containers of beer in their hands from Farrell's bar, the guys who go into the park late at night, then come out with their coats opened, weaving like they're drunk. And there's that smell again, like bacon grease, or a burning pot with no water in it.

It feels like the only thing I can count on anymore is basketball. That spring, we seriously practice every day. Tina makes it to the schoolyard around four thirty. Diane gets there maybe an hour later. I'm there from about four. It only takes me maybe forty minutes to get home from school, ten minutes or so to do homework, five to change, maybe run to the grocery store for my mother—though it's starting to annoy me. She's home all day. Why does she wait for me or Bobby to come home to get the food shopping done? What's she doing all day?

School's almost over, and the summer will be my time to up my game. I'll play every day, morning until night. Somebody's always in the schoolyard. Downtown where we used to live, there was no schoolyard, just an indoor gym with a ceiling that seemed to be right over your head. They locked it after the games and opened it only for official practices of the boys' team. The girls only got to use it during the once-a-week gym class, and nobody was showing us how to play the game.

It was always empty looking, where we used to live. Downtown, just past the Brooklyn Bridge, is where the big stores, like A&S, Korvettes, and Woolworth are, so after six, it looks like nobody lives around there. But on the side streets, past Livingston and Fulton, there are little stores with apartments above them. Tucked away are blocks with stoop houses with rickety steps and broken mailboxes. That's where we lived.

Our new neighborhood has no big stores, and the central parts of its geography are the church, the school, and the schoolyard. From Prospect Park West and Prospect Avenue, the streets slope down, so you're either walking uphill or downhill from the avenue. The school-yard is like a surprise coming out of the ground—it was built about two stories down from the street. The fence around it covers half of Prospect Avenue and fully half of Howard Place, which is a beautiful block across from the school. It has porch houses, trees, and always makes me think I'm in Ohio. I have no idea what Ohio looks like, but this is what I imagine. Plus, you can get in this huge schoolyard only from the one entrance on Howard Place. So, for me, coming from the avenue, I have to walk almost all the way around the schoolyard before I can enter it. This way, I know who's in it, if there's a court empty, and whether or not I'll be able to play immediately or have to wait for a court to open up.

Once you're in the schoolyard, the street level is two stories up on the Prospect Avenue side, but it's even with the Howard Place side. Amazingly, it's hard to see the houses right across the street because of how many trees are on both sides. What it ends up feeling like is being in some separate world from the neighborhood. The back of the church is one whole side of the schoolyard, which also feels like a big protective wall. Even if someone is watching from outside of the fence, they're not immediately visible to us in the schoolyard.

I'm playing Kings with Tina and Diane. Tina and I want to be roving forward when we make the team. We can play both sides of the court then. In girls' rules, only two players can rove back and forth. Boys' rules let all the players go back and forth. I practice dribbling because that's the key skill for a roving forward.

So Tina, who can be a real pain because she acts really spoiled, makes up a rule where we only have three seconds to shoot after we catch the ball. This is tough because in Kings, you have to catch the ball with only one hand.

We start running around like crazy to keep up with each other. Tina's father is watching from the Howard Place side of the schoolyard, like he does every day before supper. I'm just about to shoot, and Tina says, "Was that your brother in the paper yesterday?"

"What?"

"Was your brother in the paper?"

"What for? Who?"

"It was about drugs. It had your brother's name and your address."

I open my mouth but have no words. I'm standing straight, but I feel like I just fell down. I bounce the ball, hard, over to her, even though it's not her turn. I run out of the schoolyard, around the corner, up the block to the avenue, and home. I run up all two flights of stairs and keep running down the hallway until I'm in the kitchen with my mom.

"Was John in the paper yesterday?"

"Who said that?"

"Tina Mongielli. Was he?"

"What did she say?"

"She said it had our address and his name."

"Does Tina read the paper?"

"I don't know! I don't care! Was he?"

"How did she know about the paper?"

"Ma, just tell me! I want to know."

"All right, all right now. Yes."

"Why didn't you tell me? What did it say? Do you have it?"

"Just take it easy, miss. I gave you the answer. You don't have to know everything."

"Please let me read it, Ma. I just want to read it." I'm so mad I'm crying.

She doesn't say anything. She leaves the kitchen and comes back with the paper.

It's on page four of the *Daily News*. The headline says, "NAB 7 IN BROOKLYN DRUG HEIST." It's all about downtown where we used to live and how this was the first arrest in a big police crackdown on drugs. The police chased a green Plymouth DeSoto—John's car—up to Twelfth Street and Fourth Avenue. Then they let it go, but another car followed it to an apartment on Fifth Avenue. They arrested seven people in the apartment. They gave the names and addresses of the arrested people. I know three of them—Julius Santiago, Leroy Phillips, John Joyce.

I give the paper back to my mother and sit down across from her at the kitchen table. She gives me a can of Coke and opens up a can of beer for herself. It's early still.

"Is he going to jail?"

"That depends on what happens."

"Where is he now?"

My mother is crying, but she doesn't have tears. "He's in the hospital."

"How come? What happened?"

"There was a fight during the arrest. They beat him."

"The police? Is he hurt? Did you see him?"

"We were there all day today. Your father and Martin and I. He's all bandaged up. His lips are all swollen. It's a concussion. But he's going to be all right, thank God."

"Is anybody at the hospital with him now?"

"No. We had to leave after they let us see him." Now the tears come—a lot. The beer glass hides her face when she takes a swallow.

"But you said he was all right. He's all right, isn't he?"

"He spoke to us. He's very sorry. He has to rest."

"Does he still have to go to jail if he's in the hospital?"

"I don't know. Yes. We'll see what happens."

SECOND QUARTER
1970=1971

TRAVELING

I t's Christmas Eve, and we're going to visit John in jail—Sing Sing, Ossining, New York. Bobby and I ride in the back seat, the both of us held captive by images of branch, stone, sky, going in the other direction. Our mother and father—the both of them, together—ride up front, not talking. It's supposed to snow.

"Kate, crack your window a little to get the smoke out," my father says.

She does. It is immediately freezing. Bobby, whose seat is behind the front passenger, my mother, looks at me as if it is my fault. I got sick once in a car a million years ago, and nobody ever forgets it. But Bobby wouldn't dare complain to them—not today. Not after getting thrown out of Bishops High School for his latest infraction—smoking cigarettes. That's what my parents told me. I know it was smoking, but it wasn't cigarettes. I let them think I don't know it was pot. They need me to be innocent.

"How is the wind back there?" my mother asks, even as she is rolling up the window. "Claire, don't read. You'll get sick."

"Don't get sick in this car," my father says to nobody, everybody. The car belongs to one of his cabdriver friends.

"She wasn't reading, Jack. I was just reminding her in case she was thinking about it." My mother looks back at me as if she is examining me for signs of future criminal behavior.

I open my lips, mouth, "What?" This gets a smirk out of Bobby.

The sky looks puffy with snow just behind it. Shapes seem to be pressing down, making land feel closer to sky than usual. Up ahead, a white blob meets the horizon, and I imagine it is already snowing up there. It is especially quiet outside, a combination of the mummy sound of almost-snow and the geography of Upstate New York.

Since we left the city, there are only a few cars on the road. It's a monotonous view. Row after row of trees jut out from woods held back by huge boulders and stones, surrounding us, on either side. Every once in a while, ice clings to the branches, making them look sculptured and eerie.

My father has been upbeat, even almost in charge since we left. This is what he does—drive—and he seems to really know what he's doing about getting on highways. I hear him, but I can hardly see him over the high back of the front seats. In the rearview mirror, I can see the top of his cap. And the smoke of his cigarette drifts back here in skinny, horizontal lines. Not like my mother's smoke, which blasts through the car like we're in Vietnam and we have to run for cover.

My mother and father will be visiting John in prison tomorrow, on Christmas, while Bobby and I wait back at the motel. I imagine John in his cell wearing gray clothes, looking like himself, except he can't open the locked gate. When he first went away, I used to have cartoon bubbles in my head of him wearing black-and-white-striped pajamas and a ball and chain around his ankle. That was a year and a half ago, and this is not a freaking cartoon. This is John.

We can't ask my parents direct questions about visiting John because we'll get them nervous, and then they'll just yell at us. So Bobby and I have pretty much figured out the way it's going to work. Probably we'll stop by the prison on the way to the motel for visiting hours. Kids are allowed to visit only on Christmas, so today me and Bobby will wait in the car. Hopefully, there will be a window we can wave up to so John can see us. We only got as far as that.

"Can you put the music on?" Bobby asks.

I whisk my head over to him: *Are you crazy?*

My father doesn't make a big deal of it. He just says, "No." But my mother's shoulders wing back a little.

"Oh, man. Why not? Come *on,*" Bobby whines.

My mother starts. "Are you driving this car? Are you trying to find the exit, when it's about to snow all over the place and the road is unfamiliar? Do you think we should stop this car and break out our dancing shoes because you feel like a little music in the back seat there? Do you—"

"All right, Kate, I said no. That's all," my father says. He sounds like he's trying to be gentle, but he can't because his voice has a rough, coughing rolling in it, like he has never been able to clear his throat.

Bobby's hands are shoved inside his new peacoat, with his head against the window. His eyes are slits. I peek at him now that my mother has been startled into one of her nervous machine-gun ravings. Bobby doesn't remember to gauge whether her reaction is going to be immediate, or whether it will take some time for her to become hysterical. I'm so much better at timing her than he is. But she is much, much more loving to him than to the rest of us.

Here it is; here comes the snow. We are surrounded by little tiny flakes in hundreds and thousands of swirls. "Bobby!" I say, shaking his arm. "It's snowing."

"Cut it out!" Bobby swings and punches me, hard, in my shoulder. I scream and lunge for him across the inches that divide us. I am punching his head and neck. He grabs my arm and twists it up my back. It goes beyond regular hurt. He keeps twisting, twisting. I am begging. God. God. Stop.

My mother is halfway into the back seat along with us, her arms tearing at Bobby. He lets go. I curl up into my side holding my shoulder and arm. My mother is chanting, "What is wrong with you? How can you hurt your sister like that? What is wrong with you?"

Bobby's reason is that I woke him up. I startled him. I think I can do whatever I want. I am a spoiled brat. He hates me.

My father opens the window, spits, closes it. "I won't have this goddamn behavior in this car, do you hear me?" he shouts. In the mirror, I can see how red his face is, and we are all stunned at how mad he is. "You keep your hands to yourself, boy, and you stop with all the chatter, miss. Goddamn kids."

I have made things worse by forgetting to think before I act. I forgot that Bobby can't take sudden movements; I forgot that I can't win a fistfight with him.

"I'm sorry," I say, forcing myself, my head against the window.

Bobby is crazy, and I am the only one in the car who knows it. If I can bend my behavior around him, I am safe. The long quiet softens the pulsing inside the car. We drive forever.

After a while, my father says, "I have to stop for gas. We're almost there, but I don't want to get caught on empty."

"Maybe we can stop at a restroom, too. Claire, do you have to go to the bathroom?" my mother says. Then, as an afterthought: "Robert?"

"Okay," Bobby murmurs. I don't have to look at him to know he looks exhausted, sick. He always does after he goes crazy.

"We're stopping for gas and for a quick bathroom visit, period," my father says. "No lollygagging around."

I twist my head to Bobby, who twists his head to me. I do my lollygagging face—stick a pretend lollipop down my throat, choke, gag, panic—until I see Bobby's face cave into a mime man's laugh. We make no sound but snort one at a time through our noses. I catch my father's eyes in the rearview mirror; he winks at me.

It looks darker out than before as we drive through a turn that's cut in the middle of two lines of giant trees. They're so tall and this road is so narrow the tops of the trees seem to bend toward each other, like ladies talking over a clothesline.

My father is hunched up right next to the wheel with both hands on it, looking ahead at what's coming. My mother looks like she's ready to shovel out the whole country if she has to; she is sitting upright, one hand on the door and one hand firmly placed on the dash in front of her.

My father takes the next exit. We are slowly, slowly, moving through the sheets of snow down a deserted road, surrounded by trees and quiet.

"Up ahead." My mother points. "There's a town, and I see orange lights. Exxon is orange, isn't it?"

We all strain to see.

"It's on the right, after that church steeple—see it? It looks like that's a post office or a government office across from it. It's right up ahead," my mother tells us.

We can see the town ahead on the downward slope of the road, how it just appears out of nowhere. A bunch of dirty-white, two-story buildings in the clean snow. A frayed American flag pointing straight out, flying with its head down. Old cars half on the road, half up on a rise. Crooked Christmas lights nailed over a broken screen door. Not even one person on the street.

My father rolls up to the orange sign with no words on it, and we arrive at the gas station as if we were a boat, rocking back and forth and finally settling into place in front of the only pump. It feels like the dead of night.

The fattest person I've ever seen comes out of the office, where the windows are so dirty it's not possible to see inside. He moves toward the car in thundering steps. He wears no coat, only a plaid shirt over a big undershirt, inside the widest pair of denim overalls ever made. His hair is thin, light, wispy. His face is pink, stretched, wet looking. He could be, but he's definitely not, a fatter Santa Claus. He's not smiling.

"What do you need?" he demands.

"Fill 'er up, pal," says my completely-at-ease father. "Do you have a john we can use?"

I am not going in that john, no way. I am not getting out of the car.

"Inside." He indicates with his head. His eyes are so far apart, they could be on either side of his temples, like a great sea animal. They have no color.

"All right, let's get this show on the road," my father says.

"Come on, kids, out of the car. Let's use the toilet," my mother says, as she is opening her door and stepping out. Bobby is stepping out too. My father is already out. Snow is slanting down at them.

"It's okay, I don't have to go," I say. And I don't, or at least not much. I can hold it. I don't care how much farther it is to the prison.

My mother bends into the car. "Come on, now. Let's go inside together and then come back out together." I know what she means, but I can't move. She thinks we should all stay together, and we'll be safe. I think if I don't move from my seat, we'll be safe.

"No, go ahead, I'll just stay here."

Bobby sticks his head in the front-seat side. "What are you doing? Come on."

"I'm staying here! Just go."

My mother shuts the door as she and Bobby straighten up. Her head reaches only to his shoulders. She starts inside. Bobby follows, then turns around. He goes back to the side of the car and gets in next to me.

"What are *you* doing?" I ask.

"Staying here," Bobby says, bunching his arms up under his shoulders and pushing himself against the seat, hunkering down.

I peek out at the gas station guy as he's replacing the nozzle. His eyes are blank; his face is closed. I turn to Bobby, evil on my face. There's a macaroni commercial that Bobby and I always scream laugh at. This poor fat kid is playing on the street, and his mother starts yelling for him out the window. He doesn't answer her, but then she tells him it's spaghetti day. The fat kid drops what he's doing with a big moronic smile on his face and runs home. I am making that face now as Bobby turns to look at me.

"Hey, Anthony, it's Prince spaghetti day! Come on, I got a barrel of macaroni for you! Open up those overalls, Tony, because you're gonna need more room. Anthony, wait, here's a fork . . . Anthony, take your head out of that pot of macaroni. . . ."

We are both giggling as the doors open on either side, and my mother and father look at us accusingly before they settle back in.

There's no big sign telling us that we are nearing the prison. We just reach a corner of the town, turn left, head toward it. Here, the road slopes downward to the Hudson River. We ride down this quiet, empty street until the fortress of Sing Sing rises up to stop us. It braces against land on the edge of the river. It's a hulking structure, all turrets and stone, with two tacked-on wings spreading from the center. It looks like an overfed eagle turned to stone as it was about to crash into the river.

Inside the iron-gated entry, we are directed to the parking lot. Another guard directs us to a parking space and to a tiny door. A paper sign, taped to the door, says VISITORS' ENTRANCE. My father puts the car in park, then turns to my mother.

"Bobby, Claire, let's go," she says.

"We're going inside?" I'm the first to get the words out.

"Did you think we were going to leave you in the car?" my mother says.

We get out, walk together toward the door. I feel like I am walking inside a bubble of gum. I am blinking to clear my eyes, to feel awake. My words come out slower than usual, whispery. "I thought you said we couldn't visit today."

"No, you can't, but there's a waiting room for children." My mother looks at both of us as if she just told us someone died.

"Is there a bathroom there?"

"I'm sure there is. And you'll both be together in the room. There's nothing to be frightened of," she says.

"Ma, we'll be fine. We are fine," Bobby says. To me, he says, "I have to go to the bathroom too. I'll find out where it is and take you there. Don't worry."

I want to tell them that I'm not worried. Words form in my head, but they get stuck in my throat.

My father is blowing his nose, turning away from us. My mother seems smaller than her usual five feet two inches. She stands there in her three-button winter coat, holding the handle of her pocketbook in the crook of her arm, her forearm stiffly pointed up as though she just donated blood. Her old white dress gloves, buttoned at both wrists, cover her clenched hands. She sewed a button on the left glove last night. She is wearing her old navy blue suit underneath that coat. It's always the same skirt, but she changes the blouse and puts a sweater with it sometimes to make it look like a whole new outfit. She's clever like that. My mother stands like she's always telling us to: keeping her spine straight and squaring her shoulders. On her head, she wears a small hat, really just a fabric-covered thick headband with a gathering of tiny glass beads on one side. She has short hair but a lot of it, dark black, dipped in white by the scalp. She doesn't wear any makeup, ever, on her lined, dry face. I am looking deep into her strong brown eyes, which look back from her clumpy lashes that huddle together at the corners. Her eyes are bright, clear, sober.

My father shuffles behind her as we walk. Although he was a soldier, my mother is the general in this army.

Bobby and I are deposited in a room full of brown, white, black children. When the guard calls for the visitors, my mother is the first to line up, head up, for the walk to the prisoner visiting area. Everything about her says, "It's Christmas. I'm here to see my son."

* *

Nothing is interesting in the waiting room. We don't talk to anyone, and they don't talk to us. One Spanish girl looks at me, and when I look back, she sticks out her tongue—quickly, like she's pointing. I am about to say, "What?" when Bobby tells me not to be stupid, who cares, so what? I'm not stupid, I care, and because I am insulted.

When my mother and father come back, it's unbelievable how happy they look. All the way to the motel, they talk about how John is getting transferred, and even though it's farther away, the prison offers more educational opportunities, job placement help, and has the options and potential for early release. They make it sound like John is getting a prison promotion. He's moving to Attica state prison next month, right after New Year's. Hopefully, this year will be better than last year. My family is having trouble right now with John in prison, but my mother keeps going to novenas and kneeling by her bed on nondrinking nights to say a rosary. She has faith that God will answer her prayers. I swear to God, it would be a sin if He didn't.

DOUBLE DRIBBLE

When I open my eyes, the first thing I see are the curtains of the motel room. They're stiff, gold, untouchable. The window is just above eye level. Right outside, the car is parked where my father can keep checking it. He is nervous about it because it's not his car. No other cars were parked in the U-shaped courtyard of the Red Sled Motel. The office, at the corner of the yard, is decorated like a ski lodge, with an elk-and-sled scene repeating itself in the wallpaper. The motel is sticking out on the main route, in between Croton-on-Hudson and Ossining, like a place to stop in a hurry and leave in a hurry. The Red Sled has a real Christmas tree tied to its sign in the front, with no lights or decorations, and is practically invisible at night.

It's Christmas! I swing out of the bed. Bobby is sound asleep in the next bed, but my father isn't here. My mother is laying clothes out for the two of us, the pieces all lining up as if two invisible bodies were lying across the desk, posing. I see the girl body will be wearing the tartan skirt that came in the hand-me-down bag from the "rich kids," twin girls who belonged to someone my mother used to know. The clothes never fit me in the year I get them, ever, but for emergencies, like Christmas, I can put on one of the matching outfits and get away with it. I see the red turtleneck sweater that matches the red plaid of the skirt. Now if only I was three inches taller. The style should have been a short skirt, like a miniskirt, the sweater tucked in, the opaque tights white. And if there were boots, they should be white, like go-go boots. Instead, I'll be wearing the skirt way past my knees, the sweater loose, and my regular school loafers. I hate dressing up.

Bobby just has to wear his school pants with a shirt and sweater and he's done. Plus, he can look good and fit in anywhere. It's harder for a girl. There are so many ways they can look messed up. Especially at thirteen—a lot of girls look contorted. They get boobs and don't know how to be in their bodies. Or they get their periods and act like they're dying with cramps and pain. They think about themselves too much.

I know I'm on the positive side of good-looking. Nobody ever said it; I just know it from looking around.

Bobby used to be what the girls thought was cute, but now he's even worse. Before he got thrown out, he was a sophomore at Bishops, tall, good at sports, smart in school, not a jerk. Even some of the girls I don't hang out with on the basketball team started acting all friendly to me. They'll ring our bell and call for me, out of the blue, to see if I'm going to the schoolyard. At first, when I thought it was about me, I was flattered. Then I figured it out, and I was disgusted. I play ball with those girls, but otherwise, I don't want anything to do with them.

The door opens, surprising all of us, and my father stomps in from the cold, carrying a white paper bag. "Got coffee and donuts, Kate," he says. "And here's a little bag for each of you. Sanny Claws left it for you." He says this with exaggerated eyes, stretching out the wrong pronunciation of "Santa Claus" longer than usual. Me and Bobby just stand there, holding the bags. "Go ahead, open 'em," my father says.

Inside each bag is a donut, a juice drink, and a scrunch of brown wrapping paper. Our names are written, in pencil, on the outside, in handwriting that neither of us have seen a lot, but we know it's our father's. The handwriting could have come from a little Russian kid in the first grade who is practicing writing English. I open mine first and get a five-dollar bill. Bobby gets the same. Sunday money—just like we get every Sunday on the kitchen table at home. We both always get the same amount, even though we're three years apart. It started with a quarter each and moved up this past year to three dollars.

"Thanks, Santa," I say. "Is this always what we're getting for Sunday money now? Did we get a raise?"

I know Bobby wants to know too, but he is looking at me like I just asked a stranger to fix me a sandwich.

"This is from Sanny Claws. Who knows how much the Sunday money will be from now on?" my father says, as if he really does not know. He smiles at my mother. She widens her eyes to him a little, pressing her lips together in a closed-mouth smile. Both of her dimples show.

After we all exchange gifts, we drink our juice and eat the donuts. I'm wondering if we're going to Mass, or if we have to do anything before we go back to the prison. I keep my thoughts to myself; my parents are both in good moods. Too many questions make them crazy. My mother is hustling around the room, putting things away. She seems happy.

"Can we look at a map to see how far Attica is from Brooklyn?" Bobby says as we're getting into the car.

"Next time we stop for gas, I'll see if they have one," my father says. "That's a good idea, Bobbo."

We slide out of the Red Sled Motel and onto the road that leads directly to Sing Sing. Everybody's in a good mood. My Christmas presents were a big hit: Bobby's got the yo-yo wrapped around his finger, even inside his coat pocket; my father's cigarettes are in his shirt pocket; my mother is relaxed, and her lips seem fuller with the light red lipstick. She's acting like she's glad we're not going to Mass, even though she's the one who always makes us go. John must have made her feel great about something yesterday. They said he was fine, but they didn't go into any details. They never do.

Inside the prisoner visiting room, the four of us sit around a table with John.

"How's the food?" Bobby asks.

John tilts his hand back and forth: so-so. My mother wants to know if he is eating well.

"It's fine. It's the whole day, really, broken up into three meals," John tells her. "I'm used to plain food." He winks at Bobby and me. I don't get it.

My father is sitting on the edge of his chair, like he's waiting to say something. So far, any quiet time is taken up with questions, like we're interviewing John about prison life—maybe we'd like to go there someday?

When I'm not paying attention, I'm nosy about the family at the next table. The kids are little, like four and six, the mother keeps crying, and the father, the one in prison, keeps telling the mother to shut up. The boy, who is about six, looks really afraid. He stares at his mother, then at his father, then back and forth, quickly. The younger one, a girl, sucks her thumb. She looks over at our family. I smile at her. Nothing.

My mother touches my arm, whispers, "Mind your business."

John tells us about his GED preparation, when the test is, how he's helping out by tutoring math to some of the guys in his "class." My mother and father love this. They think John is a natural teacher, since he was always the one who helped with math at St. A's and at home. Now he's doing it at Ossining Correctional Facility.

His hair is combed back, neat. He looks clean, like he just took a shower. His face is shiny. He looks like John, without cool clothes.

When he came into the room, we were already at the table. He acted embarrassed. So did we—as if we didn't know each other. He kept looking at Bobby and me—we must have changed a lot to him. Bobby grew about five inches since a year and a half ago. He's five foot eleven, and I'm five foot seven, pretty tall for a thirteen-year-old. Not tall enough to make a good guard, though. I thought I told John about getting taller in my letters? Maybe not.

"Are you playing basketball?" I ask.

"Every day," John says. "We go to the yard after work or school, or whatever, at around four. I get in an hour of basketball, usually a game, no one-on-one because there's too many guys."

"Did you have to try out to get on a team?"

John laughs, but it's not a funny laugh or even a real one. More like a long snort. "Yeah, no. Not a tryout. Just getting in there, holding your own. Like that."

I imagine John playing basketball in the prison yard. He sees me doing this. "Little Miss, the only difference is there's no refs and no time—otherwise it's just like the schoolyard," he says.

This is the last thing to worry about with John in prison—that he wouldn't get to play basketball. I imagine them all, the prisoners and the guards, shocked at how good he is, how he becomes the MVP of the correctional facility, how this allows him to get out sooner.

"Is there anything you need that we can get you?" my father asks.

John puts his head down, shakes it fast: no.

"How about cigarettes?" my father wants to know.

"I don't smoke," John says. "Did you know that?"

"Does it matter? You can use cigarettes for trading, right?"

"Yeah."

"So do you want cigarettes?"

"No."

They look away from each other.

"Well, I could use a cigarette. Give me one, Jack," my mother says.

I look over at Bobby, who secretly smokes. I wonder if he could use a cigarette. He looks like he's having a hard time keeping up with what's going on. I kick his leg. He gives me his "you're dead, just wait" look. It's not serious, though; I'm not worried. But just in case, I make my face look sorry.

The room is warm and sunny. Christmas lights blink from a wreath on the wall. There are a dozen tables set up with chairs around them. The prisoner's chair is on one side, and the other chairs are on the other three sides. At our table, John sits with his back to the wall, Bobby and I sit on each side, and my mother and father sit across from him. It feels like we could be eating dinner out. On the table is a box of donuts, a bottle of Welch's grape drink, and a bag of Wise potato chips. My mother and father smoke cigarettes. John eats the chips. Bobby and I have a donut each. Everyone has a cup of grape drink.

My mother asks John if he's reading. He tells her the title of an Ernest Hemingway book about the sun. She nods her approval. John is a "play" guy, though. He likes to read plays, even Shakespeare. He went to see a Broadway play with our Aunt Winnie once. It was about a rich man who was dying, but it was a comedy. He said it was great. My mother got him a play called *The Miracle Worker* for Christmas. It's about Helen Keller. Obviously, it's about how she is a miracle. It sounds stupid to me.

"How much longer do you have to be here?" I ask. Everyone at the table takes an aggravated breath. "What?" I say.

John says, "Looks like I'm leaving here in a couple of weeks, Claire. I'm being sent to Attica, which is farther upstate. This place is very overcrowded, and I'm on the transfer order. I have another year to be in here, but that could be shortened. So figure another year, but be hopeful maybe for six months? I'm not sure."

John always, always answers my questions with a straight answer. I love that. You ask a question, you get an answer. No big reactions, no aggravation—just the answer.

John turns to my mother. "Did you speak with the lawyer?"

"No, I left him two messages," she says. "It's the holidays. I'll speak to him, for sure, at the start of the new year."

In my head, I'm adding up the time he has been in here already—since middle of seventh grade, January 1970—almost a year. Then, if he gets out in six months, it will be June 1971. Worst case: a year, January 1972. I will be in high school! Bobby will be a senior. Martin will still be way, way older than us all, twenty-seven. John will turn twenty-two or twenty-three either in Attica or at home.

While they're talking about the lawyer, I look around without showing it. The kids at the table across from us are playing together with pieces of Lincoln Logs. The mother and father are talking in a nice way to each other, leaning in without touching. The rest of the tables are quietly talking too. There are two prison guards who stand on either side of the room, arms crossed, looking serious but not like they're mad or anything. The window of the room is about six feet above the guard's head, and the sun is pouring down on that side of the room, starting to wend its way toward the middle. It makes it warm, nice. The sun is familiar, friendly. It comes here too.

My mother is telling John a story about how Martin is "shaping up" at the local union hall. She tells him Martin reports to the office at six in the morning, where all excess workers wait to see if they are needed for the day. He always gets picked to work, she says, and the money is incredible. He's practically in the union now, she says.

"He's a long-term worker at the new building in lower Manhattan," she tells John and the rest of us. "They're starting construction on the second tower of the World Trade Center, and Martin's right in there on the ground floor. That will be a good couple of years' worth of work for him. He'll really land on his feet."

"They'll need lots of men for that job," my father says. "Your brother can put in a word for you when you get out. You can start making that construction money, while it lasts. When I got out of the service, I dug the Brooklyn-Battery Tunnel. It's good, honest work. Keep you out of trouble."

My mother nods, looking like she's ready for John to report to work tomorrow morning. Work is the number one goal in my family. If you have a job, if you're bringing money in, if you're holding your own, you're a success. Martin has been working since he was fourteen. So has John, but he has this prison interruption to get over with so he can come out and get down to the business of work. Even Bobby works. He's on a night crew that cleans the banks on Wall Street. Two nights a week, he goes in around eight and works until midnight. It's good money. All of it goes to my mother.

"As soon as I get working papers, I'm going to get a job at Korvettes or McCrory's," I say.

My mother laughs, my father raises his eyebrows, and Bobby rolls his eyes.

John looks me right in the face. "You're going to keep your grades as good as they are, and you're going to college. That's what you're doing."

Now I'm the one with the laughing eyebrows and rolling eyes, but John is not kidding.

"Little Miss, you'll get a scholarship, and if you need more money, me and Martin'll pay for you."

"All right now, that's enough," my mother says. "There's plenty of time for that and plenty of time for dreaming to be done. Let's keep our minds on what's just ahead."

John sees some invisible sign from the guard and tells us it's time to wrap it up. "Big turkey dinner being served soon," he says. "Tonight, they have some singers from a church choir giving a concert." He says this like he's got places to go, people to see.

We say goodbye standing up. My father shakes John's hand, my mother looks over to the guard for permission to pat John's face, Bobby slaps him five, and I half-wave. John keeps looking at me, then mouths one word: "college." I laugh, as if he's telling me I'm about to go on a date. He starts backing away from us, toward the door, then pretends he's playing a one-on-one game. He dribbles left, right, switches hands, hooks it toward the imaginary basket. As he walks away, he raises two fingers—two points!—so Bobby and I can fake cheer, raaaah. Even the other prisoners are shaking their heads at him. He's the man.

It's almost four o'clock in the afternoon. The sky is white clouds, no sun. The ground outside the prison is shoveled out from the snow, a maze of walkways. It'll be dark soon. We walk fast through the parking lot, four across, not saying anything, Sing Sing behind us, massive. It's cold out, so getting to the car is all we're focused on. My father has the key ready but still fumbles with the lock. We each stand, shivering, by one of the doors, waiting. He gets in, reaches over to unlock my mother's door, then mine, then Bobby's. The seats are stiff, frozen.

"We need to let this warm up for a bit before we get going," my father says.

Bobby and I have scrunched our necks to fit our heads inside our coats. I'm shaking like crazy and breathe my breath back into my face. In the front seat, they are both smoking Marlboros.

The heat makes its way to the back seat, my father puts the car in gear, and off we go. In my head, I am waving goodbye to John. As soon as we get on the main road, Bobby closes his eyes and puts his head back on the seat. I can pretend to sleep too, if they start talking.

My mother and father tell us they "started late." That means they didn't get married and have Martin, who is twenty-five, until she was "close to thirty." Now this is their life. We are their life. Neither of them ever acts happy.

New York buildings scrape out from the winter clouds up ahead.

We're about to get on a bridge, and my mother asks my father if he needs a break. If so, we can get out and walk around. My father just wants to get home. Bobby is asleep, and I am gone out the window. I wonder what is happening in Sing Sing right now. With my forehead against the glass, it's like inviting my brain into a past-life crystal ball. Nothing, not even daydreaming, can change the past. Trouble happens to John, but what does he do to always have it?

As soon as I get home, I'm going to write a letter to John. He won't be expecting it, because we just saw him. First, I'll watch *Bells of St. Mary's*, which has to be on because it's on every Christmas night. It always makes me cry.

PERSONAL FOUL

January 2, 1971
John Joyce
A-267814C
New York State Correctional Facility
Ossining, NY

Dear John,
I hope this letter finds you and the family in the best of health.
Ha ha. Sister Charles told us it was proper to start all letters this
way. Stupid, right?
*   I started this letter in school when I was doing my book*
report, and Sister Charles was making believe she was saying
prayers at her desk, but really she was sleeping. This weekend
they are putting the angel back on top of St. A's that got knocked
off when the plane crashed, and we're all coming back here to
Mass. Father Quigley is coming back to St. A's too. Why did it
take so long to get a new angel, do you think? Do you get the
paper? Remember when the plane crashed and you were, like,
ten years old, and you didn't come home until way late? Big Miss
sent Martin out to look for you. Do you think she thought you
got crushed under the plane or something? Ha ha. (Where were
you, anyway?)
*   Has Bobby told you about Bishops High School gym? The*
basketball court is beautiful. The backboards are clear plexiglass.

There's even a square painted on it, so you don't have to figure out where to hit the backboard for a basket. It's almost like cheating, right?

I told you I'm a starter for the Sunday games, right? I'm like the money—like a playmaker. The tall girl on our team always hits the jump ball to me, and I get it down to our side and set up the offense. We use a key zone—three on one side, one on the far left. I dribble the ball and pass it whichever way looks less guarded. Well, you know. Remember when I first got on the team, and the coach only put me and Tina in during the last two minutes of the game? And she only did that if Holy Child was killing the other team. Thank God for the schoolyard. Otherwise, I would never have enough practice to get better. Thanks to you, I'm a skillful dribbler. Feels like for two years, all I did was hold the ball next to my knees, crouch low, take quick, controlled bounces. Just like you showed me.

My hand is killing me now. I'll write you again later.

Yours truly,

Claire (Little Miss, but I hate that anymore)

January 3, 1971

Dear John,

I forgot to ask you: how do you like this paper? Maureen Quirk gave it to me. It's stationery for sending letters overseas, so it doesn't weigh too much. Her brother Pete is in Vietnam, and she writes to him all the time.

Everything is good, the same. Martin was home last Friday. I saw him on the way out. School is good, but it annoys me to always be the last person in the schoolyard by the time I get home. That's all the paper Maureen gave me.

Yours truly,

Claire

This is my last year at St. A's. I have a couple of friends who've been in my class since first grade, Maureen Quirk and Joyce Cantello. Once in a while, we see each other over the weekend, mostly when Maureen's parents let her have a sleepover. They live on the basement level of a brownstone a block away from St. A's. It's pretty dark and crowded in their apartment, but her parents always seem merry, with their Irish accents. As soon as you come in, they have this little table with flowers on it and a picture of President John F. Kennedy, who they are still grieving about. Maureen's parents always act like Joyce and me are "company." They like that Maureen is hanging around with the "smart" kids, which is based on our report card averages. Maureen's smart, too, but she's so nervous, that has to come first before her brain. Of course, there is zero chance of having a sleepover at my house.

I love school on Friday at two thirty. This is when Saturday feels like a big gift coming up. The classroom gets sunny and dusty because the sun moves farther west and comes around to our side of the building. We are on the third floor behind the church on the Sterling Place side. The school could be a castle owned by the losers of the war. Outside the windows, only sky and clouds show, like being in a tower. A green turret roof, from which a spire looms, seems to sit on guard, on the lookout for an advancing army. We are holed up in this room, plotting our escape through the series of corridors that connects the high school across the double-door divide on the fourth floor.

Sister Charles came to St. A's this year. This is the first time I can tell something human about a nun. I can tell Sister Charles wishes she was back at her old school.

Sometimes, on a Friday, Sister Charles will reminisce about her old school. Today she's using her old school to introduce a project. "When you have a library in the school, it is an enormously useful resource for the study of history," she says. "I had an arrangement with the librarian at St. Bonafice wherein my class met there once a week to research various topics."

We're all looking at Sister Charles, waiting to hear what this means we have to do. "History Term Papers" is written, in beautiful nun handwriting, on the blackboard. We've heard of these, but we've never had one. We know this is what she talked about at the beginning of the year when she told us about how she conducted her classes at St. Bonafice. The most important part of her story, for us, was that her students had to complete a six-page term paper on some facet of world history. As the year progressed, we hoped she forgot about it.

"Each student had a pass to spend one or more periods in the library during the lunch break," she said. "I was able to arrange my projects around the availability of books and encyclopedias in our library. Sometimes the librarian and I would even work together to create projects. It is the ideal situation when a librarian and a teacher collaborate on a teaching unit."

Here she goes.

I alley-oop my eyes over to Maureen to see how she's doing. Maureen, nervous, startled, red-faced, spends most of her day in dread or fear. She looks like she's going to cry. I sniff a little so she will look toward me. She can't see anything but this stupid future history project.

"I have been thinking and thinking about how to structure your end-term research reports, so that you will benefit from the exploration," says Sister Charles. "Since we don't have a library here, I must ask you to spend some time at the public library. There is a very nice one just by Prospect Park. Do any of you know that one?"

Most of the class is nodding, trying to reassure Sister Charles that we are aware of a nearby library. Maureen is nodding in double time, swallowing air. She's going to have hiccups later.

I am so annoyed that I can't even look at Sister Charles. I'm looking over her head, so my eyes are pointed in the right direction, but I have to work my face into the right mix of attention and worry. My head is saying, "Do we know the library by the park? Do you mean the enormous structure that sits like a pyramid at the center of Flatbush Avenue and Eastern Parkway? The grandest, best library ever built in New York? The one with the gilt letters etched down the stones, the descending piano-key entry steps that roll out and down from the triple revolving doors? The one just past Banana Hill and the park, about four avenues away from here? With the children's section, the young adult section, the research section, and the adult section on the first floor?" I am having this conversation with Sister Charles in my head. We could walk there easily; we could be there in about ten minutes. We could have a class there once a week too. Does she think we walk around our own neighborhood blindfolded?

"I will alert the librarians about your projects, so they will expect to see you," she says. "You should plan on spending at least two Saturdays there, gathering the pertinent facts."

This is taking too long. I raise my hand.

"Yes, Claire?"

"Are we going to get the assignment today?"

"Well, of course, Claire. That is exactly what I'm about to do. Was I not clear?"

"Sorry, Sister."

Maureen looks over at me like I'm hanging from a noose at my desk. I am so annoying sometimes.

Sister Charles opens a folder on her desk, consults her grade book, and asks us to pay strict attention. She drones, "Each of you will receive a topic, a description of the required elements, and a planning sheet. You will note that you each have a different topic based on what we've studied this year. I have spent a long time deciding which topic to assign each of you. I am confident that your topic will be particularly interesting to you each as individuals. When I call your name, please come up."

Sister Charles sits front and center at her desk. The sun has moved to the top of the blackboard, and chalk dust is dancing around with the amoebas over Sister's head. It is so quiet in the room only the scratchy sound of Sister's pen point is heard as she makes a final note in her book.

My eyes are closing, the blinks getting longer. Thirty students are quietly poised in the afternoon quiet, as the sun warms the room, loosening the dust to float in midair. As each student's name is called, each of us quietly walks up to the desk to receive our assignment. Sister Charles makes no comment; she hands the paper to each student, scratches in her book. I'm incredibly relaxed; given permission, I could fall asleep.

"Claire Joyce."

I follow my legs out of the desk, widen my eyes to stop the tickling burn.

"This famous person is of particular interest to your family, Claire," Sister Charles says, handing me the paper. "I'd like you to pay particular attention to Governor Rockefeller's crime program."

Paper in hand, I fold myself back into my warm desk. Why did Sister Charles speak to me about this project, when she didn't speak to anyone else? How come my family would be so interested in this subject? This nun acted nice, but there was something else, something underneath what she was saying or doing. I felt like she pulled my hair, when not even a ghost of a finger touched me as she handed me the slip of paper.

Topic: Governor Nelson Rockefeller
Write a six-page report on this famous American. Answer the Five W's in preparing this report. Conclude with your opinion of his programs, his biography, his current status. Remember to include at

least one primary source, as well as two secondary sources. Write a one-page list of all references.

Just a few minutes left on this Friday afternoon. How does Sister Charles know how much my mother hates Governor Rockefeller, or was she talking about crime because she knows John is in prison? What is she trying to say to me? Or does she just want me to shut up? I can't wait to graduate. Five months to go. My mother would have so much to say about Governor Rockefeller that I wouldn't be able to use, ever, in my report. I won't tell her about this project. Sister Charles has not done anything terrible to me, but she has made me feel wrong, somehow. But no, she is the one who is wrong. I believe me.

On the bus going home, I'm praying for John, imagining him playing basketball in the prison yard. The details of why he's there are straightforward: he got arrested for having more drugs than just one person would use "recreationally," and most importantly, he resisted arrest. He hit a cop back. He was charged with felony possession of narcotics (heroin), resisting arrest, assaulting an officer, and a few things that sound like the same thing but with more language.

Now when my friends ever dare mention him, and they usually don't, they whisper his name and make faces that are part wince, part sad, as though he were in some freak accident and is paralyzed and will never walk again. I don't know what my face looks like when they say his name, but I know that it doesn't invite them to keep talking. And we all know—me, Bobby, Martin, my father, my mother—not to say out loud words like "prison" or "Sing Sing" or even "possession." We know where John is, and we love him and pray for him every day, but we are secretive and protective about him—even from each other.

And now what? Sister Charles is going to fake point her finger at me in class like we are a family of criminals? Fuck her. Oh yes, God, I am cursing in my head. That's right, Sister Charles, you lonely nun, you slow-talking, classroom-sleeping, wish-you-were-back-at-your-old-school, not-even-smart, God girlfriend. Fuck her.

O my God, I am heartily sorry for having offended thee, and I detest all my sins because I dread the loss of heaven and the pains of hell. But most of all because they offend thee, my God, who art all good and worthy of all my love.

At first, I don't get why a man on the bus is smiling at me. We are on the Seventh Avenue bus. It's crowded. I am standing near the back, holding on to the pole. People are all around me, hanging on to the suspended handles, and here's this man leaning toward me, smiling. It takes me a second, in the slowest of slow motion, to feel that his hand is cupping the front of my uniform right on top of my private place.

I jump back and bump into the person behind me. It's a lady, and she asks me if I'm all right. Everything is running water at once, my eyes, mouth, nose. I think I'm going to pee my pants. I feel my cry face, which is a scary and ugly thing. The man moves away toward the front of the bus; I can't stop looking at him. The lady asks me again, "Are you all right?"

I shake my head. "No." She is directing people around me to let me sit down. Somebody gets up and I sit, gulping back the water in my body. I am strangled.

I transfer to the Smith Street bus, sit in the first seat on the right front of the bus. The bus driver asks me if I'm going to throw up. I shake my head. The quick ride up to Prospect Avenue gets me home, then it's just two flights up, and I'm in the door.

My mother is in the kitchen. She is talking to me, and I am staring at her, filled with vomit. I know how much she has to think and worry about. She is responsible for everything in the house—everything. If the refrigerator isn't working, she is responsible. If the landlord says he's going to throw us out if we don't pay the rent by tomorrow, she's responsible. If I tell her about what happened on the bus, she'll feel responsible. If her son is in prison, is she responsible?

"Mae Doyle is visiting this weekend," my mother is saying. "I need the laundry done tomorrow morning, please, first thing. I already went to the stores today. I'm making fish sticks tonight. Be home by six."

I wish, so crazily, that my mother was setting my hair right now.

Some nights, my mother sets my hair in rags. It's usually a Saturday, so I don't go to church on Sunday looking so plain. I sit in a straight-backed kitchen chair reading a book while she wrestles the chunks of my hair into little balls. She wraps a piece of cloth around each one and ties a firm knot right at my scalp, to keep it in place. Sometimes she hums a song, and I stop reading to listen.

My mother can have a good sense of humor, but she gets angry easily, and mostly she's not in the mood to pay attention. I like the way it feels when my mother touches my hair. Her hands are never casual. If her hands are touching one of us, it always means business. When she sets my hair, every once in a while she lights a cigarette and rests one hand on my shoulder while she takes a few puffs. Her hands are little and pudgy. The top sides are severely chapped in spots, but the palms are smooth and feel mushy. Her hands are always warm.

Nobody else is home. Martin moved into New York City to be closer to his construction job. Bobby is who knows where. John is in Sing Sing. My father is never here, but he has a good excuse.

Sometimes when my father comes home, at four o'clock in the morning, he fixes breakfast and sits in the kitchen by himself. I guess he thinks of things to do while he's sitting there because sometimes, like a terrible nightmare, there's loud hammering or banging sounds. My mother jumps up out of bed and runs toward the kitchen screaming about does he know what time it is, and does he think he lives alone. He always looks at her then, like he's confused and didn't know what he was doing. I think he wishes he did live alone. Maybe that's why he uses masking tape to fix everything. It doesn't make any noise.

My father was in the army when he was seventeen, when he was shipped off to Guadalcanal. My mother told us he spent some time in the veterans' hospital when he came home because he was shell-shocked. It means that he was very alarmed about being in the war. She says that it is something that stays with him, even though he is over it. They got married when he came out of the hospital.

My mother and father get ossified together. On those times when he's home, they'll both be in the kitchen together, and my mother will say, "Sing a song, Jack." My father sings the first few lines of some old song, swallows the last few words, then shouts, "And then we wrote."

My mother waits until he starts to sing another song, then she screams and laughs and says, "And then we wrote! And then we wrote!" I don't know what it means, but I figure it's some kind of game. The one who says "And then we wrote" is "it."

I see a letter addressed to me on the kitchen table, propped up next to the salt and pepper. I grab it and head to my room to change.

Wednesday, February 15, 1971
Dear Claire,
How are you? I hope fine. Keep the dribbling practice up. You can't practice this enough. Take a basketball, walk around with it everywhere you go for the next week. Dribble down toward the schoolyard, dribble toward the store when you go, dribble standing still, and dribble running. Don't let the ball go higher than your knees. While you're dribbling, pretend the ball isn't

there—pretend you're just moving your hand up and down, up and down. We'll talk about dribbling in a game another time. For now, just make that ball a part of your regular movement.

I haven't heard anything from you about school, except Sister Charles sleeps during class. Does she still have a mustache, or is she shaving now? Are you still the smartest pain in the (cl) ass? I read your report on World War I. A+, Little Miss. You did a good job with that—not an easy subject.

That's all for now.

Yours truly,

John

I consider answering the letter right away but know that I'll have plenty of time this weekend because Mae Doyle, my mother's childhood friend, is coming to spend the night. It'll be a drinking, crying, yelling night on Saturday—plenty of time to hole up and write John a letter. Better get outside now and start dribbling the ball. I will bounce that pervert on the bus out of my head.

FOUL BACK

February 24, 1971
John Joyce
A-267814C Block B, Cell 658
Attica Correctional Facility
639 Exchange Street
Attica, NY 14011

Dear John,

We have to do laps around the gym as a warm-up before the practice starts. As we're going around the gym, I always think, "Why are we running ourselves tired before we even begin?" It doesn't make sense. To warm up, we should pass the ball, dribble into layups, set up some shots, even play Around the World! Instead, we all gather up in a line and run around the basketball court, on the outside of the boundaries. The coach makes us do five laps. Also, if we do something wrong, talk back, say what we think, she assigns more laps for us to do.

Last week, she had me guarding instead of forwarding. I figured, okay, this is practice, it's okay. At the end of the practice, she tells Eileen Wilson that she'll start in the game Sunday, and I'll take her place as a stationary guard. I go, "Why?" The coach says, "Because I want to see how Eileen does taking the ball downcourt. Now you can do five laps."

It was the end of practice so the whole team was sitting

down, catching their breath. We were all tired and sweaty. I started running around the gym by myself, and the coach was not talking. She was just watching me run around. I tried to level my eyes to look like I learned a lesson or something, but she was looking at me as if she dared me to show what I was really thinking. I was thinking this, John: she is letting Eileen Wilson start because Eileen is older than me, and because Eileen's mother comes to the games. I really think that's the truth. I am not being a bad sport.

So then Sunday's game got cancelled because of the snow. This week, we have no game, due to the rotation schedule. Next Sunday we play one of the best teams in the league, and I already know that I'm playing stationary guard, because Mary Ann Daly told me today in the schoolyard. I did not tell anyone why I think Eileen Wilson is probably taking over playmaker. That would make me look bad. Also, it's not okay for us to disagree with the coach. We just have to take anything she says and agree with it or she makes us do laps. You never had that, did you? I see the boys' teams all the time, in the schoolyard and in the gym on game day. If the boys are getting upset about something, the coach is talking them down, helping them deal with how disappointed they are if they miss a shot, or the other team is fouling left and right, or they keep getting bad calls.

Every time I get mad about something in the game, the coach tells me she's going to bench me if I don't get a handle on myself. I'm not even going crazy! I'm just maybe complaining that somebody is fouling me when nobody is looking, or asking the coach to speak to the ref about something. I mean it. This makes me even madder, that the coach acts like I'm crazy if I get upset. Plus, I'm not even that upset—it's like I have to be all polite and calm when I say, "Coach, did you see that girl slap my arm when I was running downcourt? I wonder if we can do something about that?" Just kidding. I would never talk like that, no matter what the coach says to me, or how she looks at me like I'm from outer space. Why isn't it okay for me to be involved in the game I'm playing? Why do girls have to act so different about how they feel?

I'll be in a better mood next time I write.

Love,

Claire

Mae Doyle is here. It's Saturday night, and nobody else is home but me. They're in the kitchen. Dinner is over. I'm in the little cubby room, next to the living room, watching TV, doing some math homework. Big drinking night.

"He's a pervert!" my mother shouts to the kitchen. "He ran out on his children and his wife of twenty years! He's a no-good bastard!"

Rockefeller. She is telling Mae Doyle, and the crowd in her head, the whole story.

"Not only does he run out on his wife, but he gets himself a younger woman, with four children of her own! May the angels. It's a disgrace to everything that's holy."

I'm watching a TV show about a rich guy and his butler who suddenly have to care for the rich guy's brother's children because of a death. So this teenage girl and her cute younger twin brother and sister come to live in this huge penthouse with the uncle. But the uncle, a bachelor, pretty much leaves the caretaking to the English butler. It's stupid, but I like imagining being taken care of by an English butler. Living in a penthouse looks pretty good too.

"Oh, you're tough on crime, are you, you bastard? You'll throw a young man in prison for making a mistake, you will. But you'll let a woman leave her four children to live with you in shame and disgrace. You are morally repugnant, you are!

"You do something wrong, you own up, you pay. You take responsibility. All right. You do something wrong, you have to pay the piper. You buck up. You shoulder it. That's what my son is doing. What are you doing, Mr. Rockefeller?"

She's at a pitch that drowns out all sound in the house. Bobby should be home soon. I know better than to go into the kitchen and ask any questions. I used to do that when I was younger. Now I know—she's not looking for conversation. These screaming times in the kitchen are her talking to some other world. Mae Doyle agrees with everything my mother says.

Aside from Mae, my mother doesn't have anyone to talk to. She doesn't talk to her sister anymore because her sister said something about my father that insulted her. She doesn't have any friends except Mae, who visits and drinks with her in the kitchen. That's usually only once or twice a year, though. Mae Doyle only ever stays one or two nights, usually around Christmas or after the holidays. She is my mother's friend from childhood, and she has been shunned by her family because she became a communist. My mother told us that Mae Doyle used to hand out pamphlets down on Fulton Street about the Communist Party, and her family disowned her. She even looks like a communist—short, white hair with bangs; big glasses with magnifiers inside the lenses; roundish body; stumpy legs sticking out of black, tie-up shoes. She always wears a cardigan sweater with tissues in each pocket. My mother says she's brilliant, which is something my mother admires above all else in people.

"You're right on the money, Kate," Mae Doyle says. "The rich get richer—it's a fact. But let me tell you where the real revolution in this country is going to come from. It'll come from our prisons."

"What are you saying?" my mother asks.

"Prisons in New York are breeding grounds for political and social unrest," she says. "Read Malcolm X's book."

There is some talking, but I can't make it out. I turn the TV down low and walk toward the kitchen.

"Recreational drug users, like your son, are thrown together with men who have spent their lives incarcerated. And they're guarded over by mostly ignorant and poor men who come from Upstate New York. It's overcrowded, it's fiercely segregated, and there's more crime happening in prisons than on your worst street in Brooklyn. Just what do you think is happening in those prisons?"

I hear my mother's glass slam the table. "What in the God's name are you saying, Mary Doyle?" says the Kate Joyce who is about to break out in holy hell in our kitchen. This is quiet, almost sober sounding.

"Are you so blind that you don't know what your son is going through in that prison, Kate?" Mae Doyle shouts, who is much, much drunker than I've ever seen her. Her face is pig red, and she is sitting at the table with her legs spread and her head snapping up each time she speaks.

"Claire, get out of here right now," my mother demands in her no-nonsense, get-moving voice. I stand at the kitchen arch, looking at them. I see Mae Doyle, who has always been nice, if drunk, bringing books and albums every Christmas to Bobby and me, keeping my mother company in the kitchen when we have all given up trying, alone herself because she is without family to love her.

"What's happening to John in prison?" I ask Mae Doyle.

I get only a brief look at her—her face falling in a terrible O from her mouth—before my mother pushes me, hard, into the living room.

"What's happening to John?" I scream at her.

My mother turns on Mae Doyle, dragging her from the kitchen chair she is halfway slumped over. "Get out of this house," she whispers harshly. "Get your things, and get out of here before you're sorry. Get out."

Mae Doyle is already sorry. She is choking and sobbing, trying to stand up straight as she holds on to the archway.

"Ma, let her go to bed," I say. "Please."

"She's getting out of this house right now, this minute, and you'll be quiet, miss," she says. "I told you to leave."

"No, I'm not going! Stop throwing her around. She needs to lie down."

"She needs to go, and she'll go now." My mother is deadly calm, as if she did not drink at all tonight. Or is this a kind of drunk that people get that I haven't seen?

Mae Doyle is pulling on her coat and pulling up her rolled stockings. My mother is filling a plastic bag with the bad-smelling cheese Mae brought, and the crackers, and anything else that looks like hers. She's directing her down the long hallway, through the living room arch, past the cubby, the bathroom, just before the two bedrooms, to the door. It is almost nine o'clock at night.

"Ma, please!"

My mother looks huge compared to Mae Doyle, whose shoulders are so hunched that she could easily fall over. She is holding her pocketbook and her plastic bag in front of her, like a prayer, on her way out the door. I run to get my Converse sneakers. She might fall down the stairs!

Mae is holding on to the banister as I pass my mother, who has turned her back on her and is shutting the door to our apartment. I can't believe her meanness, and my face is screaming at her. She completely ignores me.

I walk in front of Mae for the two flights down to the street and stand with her on Prospect Park West at the bus stop. I'm at least three inches taller than she is.

"Don't blame your mother," she says.

I just shake my head, feeling awful because I am only here to get information, not because I'm really nice.

"What's happening to John in prison?" I say.

"Whatever is happening to your brother, he can handle," she says. "What your mother has to be absolutely certain of is that she spends whatever she has to spend to get a good lawyer to get him out of there. Do you hear me?" She is looking up into my face, so close I can smell the liquor on her breath.

"Stop yelling at me," I say, using the whisper-rough voice of my mother.

Mae's face performs another O. Then she turns away from me and starts walking toward Windsor Place, toward the subway. She has to go home all the way to the Bronx. This is no joke.

"I'm sorry, Mae," I say, following her. "I'm sorry you have to leave."

"Your mother won't hear what she does not want to hear," she says. She is brisk, businesslike, back a little to the real Mae Doyle. This is a relief. That person can get on the F train and go to the Bronx on Saturday night at nine. The other one could get hurt.

"I want to hear it," I say.

"Tell your mother to listen to what I'm saying. Tell her to hire a good lawyer, and see if he can make a case for your brother getting out with time served. Tell her I will help her find somebody good. Tell her it would be a terrible mistake not to do this now," she says.

"Why would it be terrible?"

"Because if they just transferred him, it means they were looking over his case and making decisions about further time served," she said. "This is a perfect opportunity for him to get the court to take another look at his case. It costs money to hire a lawyer, but it has to be done."

"We have a lawyer for him," I say, insulted that Mae Doyle thinks we don't know about lawyers.

But next time I see Martin, I am going to tell him what Mae Doyle said. That's all there is to it.

February 26, 1971

Dear Little Miss,

Don't let anyone tell you that you can't take the game seriously. You're supposed to because that's how it's played. Listen to me: you can be serious without being all emotional. If someone is fouling you, and no call is being made, point it out to your coach. But don't get all hysterical about it (I know you don't). Point it out, and if your coach doesn't bring it up to the refs, then when you go back in, foul back. Don't foul around the ball, though— it's a stupid move to slap the hand that's bouncing the ball, which I'm sure you already know. And don't move with them, either. Stand still as they are coming toward you, and just wave your arms toward one direction, then step on their foot in the opposite direction. Do you follow that? Wave your hands high in the air, move them back and forth, like you're guarding the air around the player, then step on their foot. That's one move.

Another move is when you have the ball, drive as fast as you can, as hard as you can, right at the player (the one who's fouling you). They will see you coming and will have to move toward you, or step away from you. If they step away from you, keep moving and shoot. If they move toward you, keep driving, and any move they make will be an obvious foul. If the ref doesn't call a foul, then you still have caused some damage because the player knows you're not taking any more fouls from them. Let the other player get mad. You getting mad does not help your game. Keep telling yourself that you're in the game. When you're in the game, and not in the foul, it's just like some mosquito has come around buzzing. Do you go crying to somebody in charge when a mosquito flies around your head? Only crybabies do that. Not us.

If your coach doesn't call out fouls to the ref—why wouldn't she? How stupid. Then you have to stand up for your own game.

Find ways to work within the game when it's not going "the way it's supposed to go." You get some refs sometimes who are only in it for the money they pick up on a Sunday. It's just Sunday money. They don't really care. No offense, but the refs for the girls' games are probably gym teachers or retired gym teachers. Never mind them. It's not about the refs, it's about your game. Play your game, let your teammates play their game, and win. That's all you have to worry about.

Keep cool, Little Miss.

Yours truly,

John

March 2, 1971

Dear John,

Oh man, I followed the advice you gave me, and it was great. We won, but not just because we won (though, yes, this is a good story because we won). I didn't have to foul, but I was ready to. It was the way I felt during the game. Like, I expected things not to go according to the rules, and because of that, I was calmer. Like, I knew somebody was going to walk, or double dribble, or anything. I knew the big guard from St. Ephrem's wasn't going to be able to jump as high as she looked like she could because she wasn't coordinated. I was playing the game, just accepting everything except my own bad play.

I hate when I miss shots. I know that's part of the game, but I always feel like a big hog when I shoot and miss. Like, I should have passed the ball to Tina or even Eileen Wilson, who basically just stands in her zone spot and waits for the ball. That's all she does, but she makes the shot a lot. It just annoys me how she's not running around, and how she just stands there and expects me to throw her the ball. I'm running in and out of the key, passing the ball back and forth, and Eileen just stays in one spot waiting for the ball. Tina never stands still; Diane does sometimes when she's not taking the shot herself. Okay, Eileen makes the basket at least a couple of times. So if we score thirty for the whole game (I know, ha ha), then she scores about eight points. It helps. But that's not my question. My question is, should I always go for the possible sure shot by throwing it to Eileen Wilson? Or should I take my shot, hit or miss, that's the breaks?

Thanks.

Love,

Claire

March 15, 1971

Claire,

You take the shot. But if you're not on, then you pass the ball. The shot is when you feel it's right, when your body feels like it's on its way to the basket and the field is clear, and the guard who is guarding you can't touch you. You see the angle, you know you've got the room, you stop all the thinking, and you just know. You know.

You need to know when not to take the shot, too. If the player on your team is only safe in one spot, she's not really playing the game, she's playing Around the World with some passing thrown in. Don't look at her as if she's supposed to be doing what you're doing. That's not how it happens. You see her in the corner there, and if the guards are all up on you, you pass her the ball. If she's on and she's hitting the basket, you're all scoring points. It won't always work that way; the other coach or the players will figure it out and put somebody on her. Then you have to make another play—you have to have at least five plays in your head all the time, right? Giving the ball to the corner shot is only one of them.

Do you know what a silly thing it is to act like the girl in the corner doesn't deserve the shot because you're doing all the dribbling and passing? That girl is your ace in the hole, Little Miss. Let her stay there, work your plays with the other players, and always have some way to get the right shot off. The thing you should most look for is how overly excited a player gets—the more a player is losing her cool, the calmer you should work at making yourself. You can break out, be fast, and still be calm. Play with your head. Your heart's already there. Don't be a hot-head. Those players always act like little girls (ha ha).

Talk about school next time. Which high school are you applying to?

Yours truly,

John

GOOD PASSING GAME

Martin's sleeping on the daybed in the living room. It's almost time for him to wake up from his after-work, after-drunk nap to go out for the night and go back to his apartment in the city. He sleeps in one spot, arms crossed, work boots at the foot of the daybed, fully dressed in his construction jeans and plaid shirt. He always has a crew cut, even though a lot of guys are wearing their hair longer nowadays. I think Martin looks like my father, but I can't really tell because he is so much more alive with energy than my father. My mother calls Martin a moving target, because she says he never stays still.

Plus, he doesn't just wake up—he startles awake. John and Bobby used to sneak up on him in bed, shake him roughly, and shout, "Martin!" He'd jump up like there was a fire somewhere and he had to put it out. Watching him go from a deep, snoring sleep to emergency ready was kind of funny. But even when nobody is pranking him, he wakes up like he's late for something. He also spends the first five minutes of being awake just blowing his nose. The handkerchief he keeps in his pocket is disgusting to touch. I know because I do the laundry.

"I have to tell you something important," I say to him, as he's blowing his nose.

"What's the matter?"

"Mae Doyle was here last weekend, and she said bad things were happening to John in prison."

Martin stops blowing his nose and looks roughly at me. "She said that to you?"

"No, first she said it to Momma, but then Momma made her leave—at nine at night!—and she said it to me on her way to the subway. She really meant it. She said we should get another lawyer so he could get out of there. Is that possible?"

"Okay, Claire, I'm glad you told me. I'm going to take care of it, so don't even think about it. I know what to do. I should have done this a long time ago. Okay, good, good. You go out now."

He is putting on his construction boots, smoothing out the daybed, tucking in his shirt.

"Wait. Momma went to the store to get stuff for dinner. She thinks you'll be here when she gets back."

"I can't stay for dinner. I have to go meet some people. Tell her I'll see her next week."

He's moving, I'm following. "But what about the lawyer? What about John?" I hate that I'm about to cry.

Martin stops, puts his hand on my head. "Hey, I told you, don't worry about anything. I'm going to take care of this, first thing tomorrow morning. I promise. So just stop, okay?"

I hurry up and stop. If Martin says he's going to do something, he will. Now the only worry is how my mother will react when she comes back and sees he's not here.

Bobby and I are eating dinner at the kitchen table. My mother is at the sink, her glass of beer in one hand, cigarette in the other.

"Martin's engaged," she says. The kitchen window is wide open because the kitchen is the hottest room in the house, even on this still-light-out wintry March day. I'm looking out the window from my seat because I'm trying to see if Martin looked any different an hour ago when I told him about needing a lawyer. I am stunned.

"To who?" I ask.

"A woman he met in the city. I haven't met her yet. They're going to come for dinner on Friday next, after work," my mother says. She pops another can of Rheingold, pours it slowly as she tilts the glass, calculating the head of foam.

Bobby joins the conversation. "Martin's getting married?"

"Yes. And it's about time. Living in Manhattan, working all day to come home to nobody and nothing. It's a wonder he's not deathly sick, the way he burns a candle at both ends," she says. With only a couple of swallows of beer, she is already turning slightly mean.

"What's her name? Where's she from? How did they meet?" I can't get the information fast enough.

"Hold still. Eat your dinner before it gets cold," she says, meaning that she cooked it, so make use of it. I eat, but I keep my face up, waiting for answers. The dinner is spaghetti with clam sauce—boiled water, and a can of heated-up Progresso. My mother does not eat.

"He met her through Mary Hartigan. She's a friend of hers from work. Her name is Genevieve," she says, not warming up to the conversation.

No more questions. If I keep it up, my mother will start to get annoyed at Genevieve. I have to watch out for Martin's unknown almost-wife on a drinking night. My mother is ticking. I feel her irritation. It's probably because Martin left before she got back from the store, and also because Martin's upcoming wedding is like another thing she has to do now.

"Did you see that scrimmage with the boys from John Jay?" I ask Bobby, chewing spaghetti. Ignore the most exciting news, good news—it doesn't make sense. But that's how it is.

"When is he getting married?" Bobby asks, ignoring me entirely.

"Just before Christmas, it seems," says my mother. She tilts her head back so the glass will slide the foam to one side, leaving her the clear gold of the beer to drink. "I don't know why, and I hope it changes. That's not a good time of year for a wedding. People are already spending and trying to make do with what they've got."

She gets up and moves things around on the stove. I bore my eyes into Bobby, willing him not to ask one more thing about Martin. He seems like he's in a fog, and he hasn't looked at me. Pot smoker.

"I suppose with the both of them working, they think everybody can afford to add them to their Christmas expenses," my mother says, warming up, gearing up, boiling up with anger at the nerve of her own son and this person he's involved with. I read her face like a map: the eyebrow sticking up on one side, the same side as the curling lip; the flaring of one nostril; the dimple of her cheek cutting a deep slash, as though her insides are squeezing her.

"Ma, I forgot to tell you! Forget about Martin. Did you know that they might have room for me in Holy Child? Eileen Wendt's mother is a secretary there, and she told me that one of the eighth-grade girls is switching to public school," I say. "She said they found out about it this week, and they might start calling people from the waiting list."

"Who's this?"

"Eileen Wendt. She's on the basketball team. She told me today."

"So then how would I know about it?"

"I don't know. I thought maybe they called you. Maybe they called and you weren't home."

"That's ridiculous. You're not switching even if they did call me. You only have three months of school left. You're not switching now."

"So what? I want to go to Holy Child. It's right across the street, and all my friends go there."

"Don't even consider it, miss."

"Could you call them to see if they're even looking at my name?"

"I will not. Your name has been on that list for two years. Now you're almost finished with eighth grade. It's foolish to even consider it."

"Can't you just call them to remind them?"

"What good would that do? If I call them, I'll just be telling them something they already know."

"You could tell them that I have to take two buses to school every morning!"

"You stop that yelling, miss."

"I'm not yelling! Why not just call them and find out if they can take me?"

"I am certainly not going to call them now," my mother says. "Finish eating. Let me know when you're going out." She walks through the archway into the living room, down the hallway, and into the bathroom. She takes her beer glass with her.

I get up, scrape my plate, dump it into the sink, and wipe my mouth on the dish towel. Bobby is chewing and looking at me like I'm a mental case. I walk through the archway to the living room, down the hallway, and yell at the bathroom door, "Going out!"

STOP THE CLOCK

April 12, 1971

Dear John,

Did you hear about Martin?? I can't believe it, and I even met her. She came over on Friday, and Martin sat next to her on the couch while we waited for dinner. Genevieve kept trying to get up, so she could go into the kitchen and help Big Miss, but Martin kept making her sit down. He didn't want her to get in BM's way.

Momma was good that night, though. She was calm and laughed at stuff and asked nice questions about the wedding plans. Which, by the way, they don't even really have any plans, so don't worry. Martin is not going to get married until you get out.

I bet you can't wait to get out of there. I know we're not supposed to say that to you. I won't say it anymore, but I want you to know that no matter how stupid my letters sound, I know that you are not on vacation somewhere.

Sunday's game was so crazy. We played OLPH, and we had to be in the little gym, which is so unfair because they always give the big gym to the boys. The little gym has no room for any-body, so if people come to the game, they have to stand on the outside of the boundary lines of the court. That's why the game was so crazy on Sunday. OLPH had a lot of spectators, and they were standing all the way from basket to basket on that side of the gym. If you were taking the ball out from the side, you'd have to ask people to move so you could fit in! That's so wrong. Right?

So, we were winning, and the people from OLPH—it's a real Italian neighborhood—were screaming things like, "Get the ball from number 12! Don't let her shoot!" You know that's me, right? So they're saying all these crazy things, but if we were in the big gym, it wouldn't have sounded as scary because it wouldn't have felt like they were right there, running down the court next to you. I tried to ignore them, but they were seriously right there! I looked some man in his face, like, looked right at him, while he screamed something about not letting me get past the guard. The ref called time and went over to OLPH's coaches. Meanwhile, our coach was so mad, she sent someone up to the big gym to get some of the boys' team's crowd to come down to the little gym, I guess as backup.

Well, the boys' team (Bobby's team) was finished with their game, so not only did the spectators come down, but the whole boys' team came downstairs and their coach. It was crazy. They could hardly fit, for one thing. Before they came, we had like five or six people, and OLPH had like fifteen. When the big gym people came for our side, we had almost twice what OLPH had.

Our coach told Ken, the boys' coach, what was happening, and he was so mad, he started over-cheering everything we did. So then of course the boys' team over-cheered everything we did. So you know what happened? WE STARTED PLAYING TERRIBLE!! It was way too loud, and a few of the girls on my team were so nervous they started passing at nobody, double dribbling, taking stupid shots. I hated it. Especially because the boys think we stink, anyway. They never come to watch our games, unless somebody is going out with someone, but that's only two people on my team. (Though just about every other girl wishes they were going out with someone! Ha ha.) (Not me.)

Anyway, I played pretty good, if you want to know the truth. Except one time, I was dribbling downcourt and my headband slipped off, and I bent down to pick it up, and the forward from OLPH stole the ball from me and got to take a shot. (She missed.) I stole the ball back pretty quick and got two baskets in a row after that, but Bobby is not letting me forget it. "Ooooh, my hair, where is my headband? Ooooh, here, you take the basketball, and I'll just go fix my hair!" He is driving me crazy with his stupid, make-believe girl voice, and not remembering that I got four points right after that. Anyway, we won the game, and then it was a worry that our side would get in a fight with OLPH on the street afterward. All the refs in the building came outside the school. We saw them when we left all together from the locker room. Our coach made us all leave together, and Ken was waiting at the front door with the boys' basketball team.

You should have seen Bobby, John. He wasn't mad at me or anything like that, but he looked like he was ready to kill somebody. He was looking up and down the block like wishing somebody from OLPH would say something. I don't think his teammates know how mental he is when he's mad.

When we got home, Big Miss was watching the Jerry Lewis Telethon. She told us how wonderful he was and what a good thing he was doing for those kids. I watched it a little while with her, but after "Look at us, we're walking; look at us, we're talking," when both of us were crying, we turned it off. I wonder who all of those people are who call in pledges for the show? I wish we could pledge more. Last year, I gave my Sunday money to them before the game. Momma let me call up because I begged her, and I pledged my $5. Then I waited for the envelope they said they were going to mail to me, but it never came. So I never gave the $5. Nobody but Momma knows this; she said they have millions of pledges, and some things must have gotten lost. I hope *that didn't happen to the people who pledged a lot of money. Otherwise, the totals are all wrong on the chart they fill out.*

We are always thinking about you. I'll write again in a couple of days. You can't wait, right? Ha ha.

> *Love,*
> *Claire*

April 24, 1971
Dear Claire,
How are you? I hope fine. Sounds like you're turning into a threat on the court. When you are a player that the other team is worried about, you have to keep surprising them with your play. Don't do the same thing all the time. If you always dribble down the right side of the key, change it up—go left or down the middle. Definitely fake at least twice in each game. That makes them think you are going to fake every time you start to shoot. It keeps the guards thinking ahead too much, so it's easy to confuse them. Always play the game in the exact moment you're in: if you're passing the ball to set up a play, don't be in the play. Be in the passing. That's how to keep control of the play. It makes sense.

> *That's all, folks.*
> *Yours truly,*
> *John*

I don't want to be a threat, just a solid player. I want to be a stand-up, always reliable, go-to player that my team can count on. I loved watching John play; I loved his reputation for being almost like a magician on the court. But I don't have the skills to play basketball with that kind of star quality. Plus, it's too much singling out. I like being part of the team, part of the bigger picture. I won't tell John this. He wants me to be a star.

Of all the people on my team, it's probably Tina who has the star quality. Our uniforms are standard-issue, shiny blue with gold letters and numbers, shorts with a fake skirt panel over them, and a zip-up pullover top. Tina wears the collar up and cinches the belt tight around her waist. She also wears earrings and lipstick. But it's her play that makes her look like a star—Tina explodes down the court with the basketball, tries fancy moves that don't always work but look good, and she can drive through a cluster of players to take a layup. She doesn't hold back at all. She actually gets called for fouling more than she gets fouled.

My play is more in my head. I can dribble decently, even very well. When I get downcourt, I'm happy to set up a play. To stand at the top of the key holding up fingers to signal the play feels so purposeful, like I'm directing things. If I hold up one finger, it means I'm going to pass and pick—that is, run forward toward the shooter, then stand in front of her so she can shoot uninterrupted by the other team's guard. This sometimes draws a foul, as a bonus, because the guard tries to reach over me to block the shot.

Using two fingers means I'm going to fake a pass, hand it off to Tina, then run to the other side of the key in case Tina misses the shot. That way, I'll be in a position to grab the rebound. If it's anywhere near me, nobody is usually able to take it away from me. I definitely hold on to the ball.

There are only five plays, and those plays work only if the other team uses a zone defense. If they don't and they're just playing man-on-man, I try to set up a play, but more often than not, I'm just passing, shooting, looking for who's free, snagging rebounds. I know I play this game extremely well. Even the coach, who acts like I'm some hothead sometimes, comments to the team, "Nobody is on their toes out there more than Claire. Keep your eyes on her."

I want everyone to play well, to play like it's important to them. I can't stand girls who play like it's an afterthought, or like they'll do this until something better comes along. I wouldn't be able to stand boys who play like that, either, except there aren't many boys who don't play like it's costing them something. That's why I love schoolyard play with Tina and Diane. When the three of us challenge for a court, we usually win. We even challenge boys, but they have to be a little bit younger, or maybe not from around this neighborhood, because the boys around here won't even take a challenge. They just laugh at us and tell us to "go jump rope." One of these days we will play these guys. Until then, we have to surprise the strangers of the schoolyard. I love how boys will say, "Yeah, you wanna play? Ha. Yeah, all right. We'll play you." Like they're totally goofing on us.

Then one of us—either Tina or Diane, usually, because I just can't do it—will act all girly and beg to take the ball out first. This way, we can smack down two points right off the bat, before the boys know what's happening. Sometimes the boys give up in the middle of an eleven-point game, saying they didn't want the court anyway, or acting nonchalant, like, "Have the court if it's so important to you. We weren't really trying, anyway."

But our favorite schoolyard play is when nothing else exists except the ball, the basket, the next move, the sweat in our eyes and down our backs, shots going in as if magnets were pulling the ball toward the basket, no talking, hurrying up in case some time buzzer goes off, light fading, hurry, hurry. Kings. Around the World. Twenty-one. Lightning. Horse. Nothing else exists. We're playing so hard, concentrating, that if Tina's father calls her home to dinner, we have to blink through our sweat and figure out who Tina's father is, and where we are, and how long it's been since we knew what was going on around us.

May 2, 1971

Dear Claire,

Martin came to visit last week with his fiancée, Genevieve. He shouldn't have, but I'm glad he did. She's nice. She laughs a lot. Maybe she was just nervous. Imagine when you're all grown-up, engaged, and your boyfriend/fiancé brings you to meet his younger brother in prison? I can't see you spending time laughing during the visit, Little Miss. You'd be asking nine hundred questions and wondering what all the other prisoners did wrong to land them in here. Right? (ha ha) It was really good to see them both.

I'm very lucky because I get letters all the time, from Big Miss, sometimes Bobby (but I told him he doesn't have to write—BM makes him, I'm sure), and of course, the daily reporter from the great metropolitan newspaper, Lois Lane. And who, disguised as Clark Kent, mild-mannered reporter, fights a never-ending battle for truth, justice, and the American way. Lois is really Clark, and Superman is really Lois. How do you like that? I bet you don't. You want it to stay the way it is. But things change, Lois, and you have to go with it without too much "fuss," as BM says.

Don't worry about whether you go to Bishop or St. Saviour. Just make sure you go and finish. If you study hard enough, you could get a scholarship. Start looking at college basketball teams too. Find out if any colleges have serious girls' teams. Who knows? Congress is looking at a bill that will allow girls to have equal access to sports money in federally funded programs. If that passes, you might even be able to play basketball and get college funded too. Be smart. Be good. Do your job. That's all.

Yours truly,

John

Martin and Genevieve are getting married a few months earlier than planned, by a priest from St. Thomas Aquinas, her parish, without a big wedding. Turns out, she's pregnant. Martin used his wedding money to get a lawyer from the city to look at John's case. The lawyer is sure he can get John released before the end of the year, maybe sooner.

Using the wedding and honeymoon money was Genevieve's idea. Martin picked somebody amazing to marry. I love her. I'm sorry about her wedding, but she's not. They came to see my mother and told her what they were doing, and my mother couldn't even say anything. Thankfully, it wasn't a drinking night.

I like Genevieve because every time I've met her, she talks right to me, without any phony friendliness. She's like, "How's it going?" or "What'd you do this weekend?" Regular.

The way she sat by Martin when he told my mother about the lawyer was good too. She sat upright, next to Martin, but not slumped toward him or behind him, or fading in place. She sat like she was on the seat she was supposed to be on, and that's that. When my mother protested a little by saying, "I can't let you do that . . ." Genevieve's face was sure, as if she was pointing out that the sky was above. It was a done deal.

TWO SHOTS

May 20, 1971

Dear John,

Here's a word: inscrutable. It means "difficult to fathom, enigmatic" (which means "puzzling"). If I am inscrutable, especially when I play basketball, they won't be able to figure out what I'm going to do. I heard that word on the four-thirty movie, some Charlie Chan movie, which I hate. Bobby loves those movies. Do you like Charlie Chan?

I am going to Bishop McDonnell because they are giving me a scholarship. St. Saviour, which is closer and where most of the team is going, didn't give me a scholarship. Saviour has the best reputation as a "smart" school because everybody takes precollege, academic track, and a lot of those girls go to college. They live around Park Slope, like where the brownstones are—First Street, Montgomery, around there. Anyway, it's hard to get in, so I got in, so that's good. Bishop has a commercial track and a co-op program, where the seniors work one week and go to school one week. They learn dictation and typing, and then they practice it in a lot of different jobs downtown and on Wall Street. Almost all of the graduating girls in the commercial program have jobs when they leave school. Bishop has an academic track, too, but I'll probably take commercial.

I'll be taking the Vanderbilt Avenue bus to Grand Army Plaza, then walking down Eastern Parkway past the library, the Botanic

Garden, the Brooklyn Museum. Bishop is right by there. It really is a beautiful school from the outside. I haven't been inside it yet, but I like that it kind of mimics the architecture of the library and the museum, which are both in that white stone called "limestone." Bishop takes up almost half the block, with a big staircase main entrance and three huge doors. It's beautiful. They don't have a basketball team, but neither does Saviour. They play intramural against each other, or maybe some other school? I don't know.

Miss Benedict, my coach, said she's looking into getting a girls' high school league going. The program at Holy Child only goes up to eighth grade, so I can't play on the team next year. It's a matter of available coaches, other parishes who have a program (none do), and how many girls they will get to sign up. I don't know how she's going to do this, but she's trying, and she means what she says, so it's a possibility. Miss Benedict has the whole team over to her parents' house on Terrace Place every Friday night. She serves soda and snacks, we play games like Password and charades, and she even has a piano that some girls know how to play. I really like Miss Benedict because she's kind of mean, like you definitely wouldn't mess with her, because she is "the boss," but then she has everyone to her parents' house every Friday. She isn't even that friendly when we're there, but she looks relaxed. Sometimes she looks so mad and tense. She is definitely not inscrutable. She just means business. I like her because she's really fair. Plus, she goes right up to the refs, no problem. She is scary, which I also like about her. She doesn't get hysterical or start yelling. She goes over to the refs like, "Okay, enough, look what's happening." The refs always pay attention to her. She's got us covered.

What about you? Do you ever write ANYTHING about yourself? Inscrutable?

Love,

Claire

There are court dates, meetings, and phone calls among my mother and Martin and Genevieve. My father is even on the phone one time with Martin, telling him he has some money for him. My mother stands right next to the phone, ready to grab it back quick, as soon as my father finishes his few words with Martin. Then he slowly walks down the hallway, out the door, to work. That is the place he goes, daily, consistently, without too much goodbye from anyone. There is money on the table every morning that my mother uses to take care of everything. It's not a lot, but it's there every day. She can count on it.

I am told to stop worrying, take care of my own business, and wait to hear the news about John when it's ready to be told.

Martin and Genevieve get married on a Friday evening, in the rectory of St. Thomas Aquinas, then they have a few people over to the back room of a bar on Thirteenth Street. Her family is nice, but we sit on one side of the room, and they sit on the other. It's too bad John can't be there. My father takes the night off. My mother acts all nice, like the mother from *Leave It to Beaver*. Bobby sneaks drinks from the open bar. It's over in two hours. They move into the top floor of a brownstone three blocks away from us. My mother tells me not to even think about going over there without being invited. Genevieve tells me to stop by anytime. For now, I'm taking my mother's advice. I don't want Genevieve to think we're a bunch of no-manners, no-consideration hillbillies.

I heard Chris Doyle call Billy Mooney "shanty Irish" the other day in the schoolyard. I never heard that before, but I immediately knew what it meant. It made me stop and think about if we are in that category. I'm thinking no. I think shanty Irish doesn't even know it's acting low, or that some things are not done. Like, it might be considered shanty Irish to share a dish towel around the table instead of a napkin. My family does that, but we don't do it if somebody outside the family is in the house. Like, we never share a dish towel when

Genevieve eats dinner at our house. We know it isn't polite. So that cancels us out as shanty Irish, according to me.

The description fits Billy Mooney, though, sadly. His mother and father fight in the street, and his father beats him up in the street too. They all drink, and they do it out loud, without any shame.

June 1, 1971

Dear Little Miss,

You're right. I don't say anything about myself, because there is nothing to tell. I have a monotonous day filled like this: school, eat, work, one hour in the yard, work, eat, read or write, lights out. There is nothing to tell, and there is nothing to worry about. The most exciting thing I do is read, and you wouldn't like what I read because you don't like science fiction. But you should read science fiction because it's fantastic. Get it?

Oh, and yes—it is really getting very hot in here. It looks like I will be getting out sometime in July, so that's a break. I'm not even kidding about how hot it is. That's my big complaint. Let's see: did that help? So now you know why there is not much news coming from here. End of report.

Good luck on graduation. Tell me all about it.

Yours truly,

John

June 15, 1971

Dear John,

Today I will report on the graduation. We took the bus together, me, Momma, Bobby, Daddy, down to St. A's. It was a long graduation, with speeches, medals (note: I didn't get any; Alexander Imperlozzono got the English medal. Maybe because I lost the spelling bee in the Herald-Tribune contest?), then everyone got their diploma, and out we processed.

I'm not supposed to be disappointed about the English medal, Big Miss says. I am not disappointed. I am mad. Here's why: every week, Sister gave me back a book report with an A+. Alexander Imperlozzono even commented once about how I never get anything lower than that. He must have been keeping score. I was too, though, to tell the truth. I know who gets the good grades, and I know who is good in what. Of course, Anthony Conforte got the math medal and the all-around academic medal. But I can't believe that out of everyone in our class (there are forty of us), it was Alexander Imperlozzono who got the English medal. He even looked at me on his way back from the altar, but I didn't look at him because Joy Knight and Maureen Quirk were looking at me with sad faces, and I wanted to shout at them to cut it out. I just kept looking at the crucifix on the altar, remembering sad stuff about Jesus. Also, if you get the English medal, it doesn't help you get into high school, because you already got into high school, right? It's just about making your parents proud of you, or something like that. They were proud enough and couldn't wait to get out of there.

We went to eat at the same bar Martin and Genevieve had their reception at on Thirteenth Street, except we just sat at a table near the bar and had sandwiches. We even had dessert. I'm glad it's over. Getting medals and all that on the last day just makes everyone feel bad.

The summer league is starting next week after the communion breakfast, which will be the last communion breakfast for the eighth graders on Holy Child. Everyone gets a trophy, but then they announce MVP for each individual team. There are six boys' teams and one girls' team. The boys go all the way up to

college summer league. The summer games are always exciting,
and you will be able to see them too!

I'm tired now. Write to you tomorrow.

Love,

Claire

What I don't tell John is that Sister Sean Maura, who is not even my classroom teacher, came over to me as we were lining up to process into church, bent down, and whispered in my ear, "Say a prayer for your brother John when you're in Mass today." It's not that I minded Sister Sean Maura's concern, it's that everybody around me heard her whisper it—Irish whisper.

I never act ashamed, and really, I am not ashamed of John. I'm really, really sorry he's in prison. It's nobody's business, and that's why I don't talk about it to my friends. None of us talk about family or anything like that. Maureen Quirk's older sister is always going out with different boys, and she has a reputation. I would never say anything about that to Maureen. She knows it for sure, and some older guys have said stuff that's almost dirty to Maureen, but she was with me when they did that, and I have a hate face that will shut anything like that down in one minute. Also, I have brothers. So nobody would ever. Still, my friends totally understand and get that family business is private.

June 24, 1971

Claire,

Forget about the kid who won the English medal—he needs the English medal so he can learn how to spell his last name. Ha ha.

So you're out of St. A's, the last Joyce to get caught smoking, cutting, writing on the bathroom walls. Wait a minute. You didn't do any of that? What a girl you are.

Are you running for office, or driving a truck, or teaching college this summer? Oh ho, you say, that's not possible for a thirteen-year-old girl with no English medal. Sorry, you'll have to get to the back of the line. What? Did you say you were wait-ing in that line already? Well, nobody here saw you. Did you see her? I'm sorry, Miss. You'll have to get to the end of the line. We only serve Entenmann's cake to English-medal holders.

You crack me up, Claire Joyce. Little Miss, go shoot some hoops.

Yours truly,

Alexander Imreallyaloseronno

June 28, 1971

Dear John,

Here's a book report about the communion breakfast, starting with the title:

"Claire Joyce wins MVP at Holy Child."

Yes, I did! This was not a definite thing. I did not go in there thinking, I'll get this. And the coach, Miss Benedict? She acts like she half hates me, anyway. But she half hates everyone, not just me. She would definitely half hate you. Ha ha.

It's a nice trophy. Big Miss couldn't wait to get out of the breakfast, but she was happy for me. She would have been hap-pier with the English medal. I know, I know. I'm just saying it because it's true. I am happier with this MVP.

I'm not just happy. I'm gloating. I know, I'm not supposed to enjoy it so much. So what if I am? What's wrong with that? Just telling you, who taught me everything I know. Thank you. I hope Miss Benedict is able to get a summer league. Do you believe that Tina and Diane are both smoking cigarettes? They buy a pack together and hide it in Prospect Park, then go smoking after dinner. Isn't that stupid? Tina is also wearing a pocketbook all the time, but she looks like she's going to pass it or dribble it, so she doesn't realize how moronic she looks holding a handbag on her way to the schoolyard.

Summer is definitely here. Benny's ices is open, school is out, basketball every day. Babysitting for some little kids on Sherman Street, whose parents go out with each other every weekend. They own the whole house, and the kids are kind of brats. It's fine.

Can't wait until you get home.

Love,

Claire

REBOUND

John is supposed to get home on a cloudy, humid day after the Fourth of July weekend. I'm in the schoolyard, with one eye on our fire escape. My mother promised she'd put sneakers out there when he came home, so I'd know.

Nothing, and it's already four. I'm dribbling the ball, protecting it from Tina, who's trying to steal. We're waiting for an open court. She's still a better dribbler than I am, but she's a hit-and-miss shooter. Plus, she's a few inches shorter than I am. She's all over the court, though, in a game, bursting around with the ball. I'm not so exciting. Bill Bradley's not so exciting, either, and he averages fifteen points a game for the Knicks.

A court opens up and we pounce. Whoever throws the first ball in the basket wins. Up, easy, swish—I win.

Three girls from St. Saviour challenge us for the court. It's me, Tina, and Diane. We've seen these girls a few times but never played against them. I'm about to go to Bishop, Tina's about to go to All Saints, and Diane goes to St. Edmund. The other girls don't know that we played for Holy Child, or that our whole life consists of playing basketball.

Diane takes the ball out, passes to me. I pass to Tina, who dribbles around the girl guarding her to fake a shot, and passes it to Diane. Diane is underneath, left side, completely free. Point.

Half-court game: I take it out, bounce vault it to Tina, who chest passes to Diane, who hands off to me as I'm coming back in from out of bounds. I dribble out two strides, draw the guard, dish it off to Diane, who is under the basket, right side, completely free. Bang.

When we're stupid, we think our shot is the only answer. One of our exercises during official practice is to constantly pass the ball, looking for the open person. If we are without guards, have a beat to set up a shot, and are near the basket, then we're allowed to take the shot. And it better go in. The coach always says we have to play smart. Eyes out for the open player. Hold back, measure up, break out. This game is designed to match up with how my brain works.

In twenty minutes, we kill them, 21–10. We're not overjoyed; we're relieved and happy to have had the practice. Then we start really practicing.

I've forgotten to look at the fire escape window, but I look now. John is standing on the high side of the Prospect Avenue fence, smiling at me. I start to run out of the schoolyard, but he raises his hand and indicates he'll see me later. I don't know what to do, so I just stand there. John starts walking up toward Prospect Park West, almost gone. He's wearing a cutoff short-sleeve sweatshirt, tan pants, and sneakers. I look up toward the fire escape—nothing there. Even though I lost time during the game, I'm mad that she didn't put the sneakers out there when John came home.

As soon as he's out of sight, I run out and up toward the avenue. He's already getting on the B75, going somewhere. I watch him walk to the back of the bus, just a guy on a regular day. What about the party we had planned? We were going to have dinner, have a cake. Martin and Genevieve were coming over. I run home.

My mother is sitting in the kitchen, beer in hand. From the look of it, there's been a beer in her hand for a few hours. She says nothing to me; I say nothing to her. I stare at her for a long time, but it might be only five minutes. I don't feel teary or sad—I feel murder.

No words are necessary. John came home, took one look at our mother, sized up the situation, and left. End of story. Welcome home.

* *

I see him the next morning, sleeping on the daybed Martin used to sleep on. I'm being really quiet because I have no idea what time he came home. He wakes up anyway.

"What time is it, Claire?"

"That's the first thing you say to me?"

He laughs, jumps up out of the bed, starts doing squats. "Ten-hut, Sergeant. Private Joyce reporting for duty, sir."

"What the hell?"

"You curse now? That's what you say to me?" He is twisting, doing opposite-leg toe touches.

It's stupid, but I feel a little shy. I just smile at him, waiting for him to complete this crazy routine. My mother opens the front door, comes in with bags from Entenmann's bakery and the supermarket.

"Oh, good boy, you're up! I'm making a nice breakfast." She's got that morning-after-drinking attitude of making it all better.

"Great, I'm starving," John says.

"Where did you go yesterday?" I ask him.

"Downtown, saw some friends, hung out, asked around about work," he says, doing knee bends.

"Did you ask Martin?" my mother says, emptying the bags on the kitchen table. "He should be able to get you on the shape-up list for construction."

"No, I'm not going to do construction," John says. "I'm going to look for a job on Wall Street."

"Wall Street? What will you do there? You don't know anybody there," my mother says.

"I'm looking into it, don't worry. When is breakfast gonna be ready? Do I have time for a shower?"

He's been home for exactly a half a day, and she's already making him feel like he has to hurry up and get a job. Shouldn't he hang out a little bit, or just go play ball? What's the big hurry? I put these questions into my facial expression but don't say anything.

"Little Miss, I need a shirt ironed. How much are you charging?"

"I'll iron it for free as a welcome-home present," I say. Man, I forgot that I had a bunch of Sunday money from John because he always asks for something to be ironed.

He hands me a white shirt and a tie and heads for the bathroom. The shirt is definitely something he would wear on a job interview— is he going to Wall Street today?—so I get the water squirter and set up the ironing board to get to work.

Bobby comes out from the bedroom he shares with my father, and then even my father gets up and shuffles out to the kitchen. My mother is frying bacon, perking coffee, scrambling eggs, and basically acting like the restaurant is now open for business. John's home. All is good in the world.

John gets a job in, like, five minutes. Seriously, by the end of his first week, he is reporting to 11 William Street in the operations department of some new payroll business. He says it's all about making money. He likes that, and he thinks he wants to learn how to do that. He says they will pay for his classes if they pertain to his duties. He does shift work, which means his schedule changes every week: sometimes he works a regular nine-to-five; sometimes he doesn't go in until six at night and works until two in the morning. He says he likes that. He seems happy to be on Wall Street. We are all happy for him. The summer is good. Things are good. I'm making money too, ironing shirts for John every day. It's not much—fifty cents apiece— but it's adding up.

* *

I spend every day playing basketball. Directly across the street on Prospect Avenue are row houses, each three floors high. This is where Tina and Diane live, next door to each other, each family living on all three floors of their house. I can't even imagine it; I've only been inside the hallways when I call for them. Nobody goes in each other's houses. The mothers don't want it. They want us outside.

Almost every day, John walks through the tree shade of Howard Place on his way home from work. When he gets to Prospect Avenue, the high side, he leans against the fence for a minute to watch me play. I don't look at him. But I show off my most serious playing when I know he's there. Even if it's just a scrimmage or a warm-up, I'll start stealing the ball from whoever's dribbling, dipsy doo toward the basket, cut a layup. If I miss, I blame my sneakers by looking at them with a mad face. If I make the basket, I don't even smile. I act like there are bigger things on my mind, like hooking or jump shooting. I've been practicing jump shots, the one where you pause a second in the air before you take the shot. I can't do it. It looks so great, but it's way hard to do. Nobody can do it on the girls' team. But we make believe we can, or that we will be able to do it any moment now. John is gone by the time I sneak my eyes in his direction. It's near six, time to head home. The schoolyard quiets down at this time every day.

I used to wonder what it would be like to go to a different house, a different life, on the way home. Would I want to be in the houses across the street on the Howard Place side, shaded by trees and covered porches, with pumpkins on the stoop and plants in the window? Or would I want to cross the avenue and head into one of the three-story houses where one whole floor is for the bedrooms? Would I have a room of my own, and a desk, maybe even a fish tank? Posters on the wall? A closet with more than three outfits, a dresser with a mirror and hanging necklaces dangling from the crevices? A fluffy rug on the floor and maybe a pillow big enough to fit my whole back as I lean against my bedpost, talking on a princess phone? No—the phone is too much. I don't even have anybody to call who doesn't already live at my house.

By the time I pass the pizzeria, at the door to my building, I'm ready to go home. Having a room in a house that offers those kinds of luxuries would take too much effort. I would have to be a girl who fits that picture. That is definitely not me. It would take too much imagining to give everyone different lives to fit new roles. It's hard enough to figure them as they are in real life.

When I get home, John is fighting with Bobby.

"What do you think you're doing? Do you think you're being smart?" John yells at him. "Don't lie to me, man. I see how high you are."

"Don't be a fuckin' dick, shithead," Bobby yells back.

John moves up to Bobby's face with his whole body but does not touch him. He has to look up a little because Bobby is taller.

"Call me a shithead again and I'll put you through the wall," John says, not loud, but scarily. Bobby backs away; he is not stupid. John does not fool around when he is mad. Anybody would back down.

My mother comes in from the kitchen. "What's going on?"

"We're having a political disagreement, Big Miss," John says. "Bobby is on his way to becoming a Republican, and I'm trying to straighten him out."

"What? Robert Joyce—oh, stop this nonsense." My mother gets that this is so out of the question that John has to be kidding. She goes back to the kitchen.

"Claire, get lost," John tells me. I don't want to be bossed around, plus I want to know what they're fighting about, so I just give him a who-do-you-think-you-are face and stay in the living room. He lets it go.

"It's more than weed, Bobbo. Seconal? Tuinal? What is it?" John asks.

Bobby looks over at me like he wants me to leave. I am already getting off the chair because I'm relieved someone is talking to Bobby about how messed up he is becoming. He's turning into a "down-head," which is what the people who hang out on the parkside are called. Those guys, and there's even some girls, sniff glue, smoke pot, and take pills that make them fall and bounce into things. Bobby's friends all hang out there.

I hear John talking about "where this is leading" on my way down the hallway. He should know. Is knowing enough to fix the problem, though?

I am the weird one, I secretly think. The whole neighborhood is smoking pot, drinking, trying other stuff like acid and ups, downs. One night in the schoolyard, this kid had a little piece of cloth with a netting over it. He and his friends stood over by the entrance to the boys' school, cracking it in half, then sniffing it hard. They called it "snappers," but the real name of it is amyl nitrate. The boys went from hanging out by the doorway to running around like crazy, laughing, breathing heavy. It was like their blood began to circulate at warp speed, like on *Star Trek*. Then it was over.

The downheads take pills, and they weave around, kind of off-balance, eyes half-closed, mouths open. Potheads are usually cracking up over something, going for a snack to either Lewnes, or no-name-luncheonette. Sometimes the downheads smoke pot too, but it doesn't change what they look like. Maybe they smile their mushy smiles more.

I feel like it is all an inch away from my next step. Like, it is going to happen, and I'm just prolonging the time. Even Diane and Tina smoke pot. They do it on weekends, over in Prospect Park. They're both wearing makeup too and not always up for going to the school-yard. And it happened, like, overnight. Tina and I graduated, we had the communion breakfast, played a few games in the schoolyard one week, and then *poof.* They were girls who were walking to the park, wearing mascara, smoking pot—like it was natural.

* *

John has been home for two months when Attica prison becomes news all over the TV and the newspapers. None of us goes out for four days—I even stay off from school on Thursday and Friday. John isn't there at Attica, but we feel like something horrible is about to blast down the door to our house. My mother doesn't even drink.

The prisoners at Attica have taken over the prison, people are getting killed, and the whole prison is in an emergency situation. Everyone in the whole world is looking at it.

John says, "Good for them. Good for them. Good for them." He looks sick and happy, at the same time. He's working at his new job at a brand-new company on Wall Street called Automatic Data Processing. As soon as he walks in from work, carrying the newspaper, he sits down in the cubby room with me, my mother, and Bobby and watches the news. Martin comes by every night, and even my father watches the news as he drinks his coffee getting ready for work. My father keeps muttering, "Goddamn it, goddamn it." Martin blows his nose a lot, looking almost joyful about how John has "dodged that bullet."

I want to know if John knew any of them. He shakes his head. "There were guys who were trying to get petitions signed, about the facilities, how crowded it was, all that," John says. "Mostly Black guys, Muslim guys. You wouldn't understand."

We aren't allowed to ask him any further questions, and we stay quiet in case he wants to tell us anything. Fat chance—he never talks about anything. I bet Mae Doyle knew all this already; she's never coming back to our house again, for sure. My mother wouldn't have it.

We learn from the papers that the prison is "wildly overcrowded" and that almost half of the prisoners are under thirty years old. The reports say that the prisoners are angry about the death of a prisoner in California. It's a political statement, the news says. One of the demands is that they be transported to a "non-imperialistic country." Before I heard that, I hoped they had a chance to get better conditions.

One of the things they want is release without parole. John already has that, and he got out even before he was sentenced to get out—almost one year early. Every time Governor Rockefeller is on the news, my mother clucks her tongue, sucks her teeth, and looks like she is going to spit right on the floor.

He refuses the prisoners' demand that he show up at the prison. "That bastard started all this," my mother says. "How many young kids are in that prison that shouldn't be? They're not the trouble-makers causing this riot here—God bless them, they're probably so frightened." In my mother's eyes, anyone who is in there for having drugs on them, like John was, should never ever have been in these maximum-security prisons.

She says the rosary every day for four days straight. By the time Monday morning comes around, I'm ready to go back to school. My mother asks me to stay home. "I don't want you on Eastern Parkway if things go terribly wrong, Claire. There's no chance things will end well there," she says.

Two hours later, the news is reporting that the yard where the prisoners and hostages are was stormed by state police using tear gas, helicopters, guns. There are no pictures on television, but we imagine dead bodies all over the yard. What is happening to our country?

John doesn't come home until two o'clock in the morning, wear-ing the body he used to wear before he went to prison. I hear him come in, and I run to the hallway, along with my mother, to see him. He has that wet smile and bent-shoulder posture. My mother puts her arm around his back, tells him she's glad he is home, does he want something to eat?

THIRD QUARTER
1974-75

DENY THE BALL

October 4, 1974
President Richard M. Nixon
The White House
1600 Pennsylvania Avenue, NW
Washington, DC 20500

Dear President Nixon,
I'm writing to you because it's an assignment in my AP history
class. We're supposed to pick a world leader, living or dead, and
write to them trying to understand their decision-making pro-
cesses given the context of the world they live in. I'm not sure
we're supposed to mail it, but I'm mailing it. Why write a letter
if you're not going to send it? Hopefully, the people at the White
House will forward it to you.

Since it's probably not going to reach you anyway, I could
have written to a dead leader—the chances of a reply are just as
slim. Just so you'll see where I'm coming from, if I chose a dead
leader, I would have written to John F. Kennedy. I'm interested
in presidents of the United States, obviously.

First of all, thanks for getting us out of Vietnam, even
though you announced it when I was in seventh grade, and
I'm now a senior in high school, and American troops are still
in Vietnam. The New York Times reports that there have been
more than twenty thousand soldiers killed from 1969 until

today. That's not counting the troops that died since 1965. The Vietnamization policy you instituted, according to my history teacher, was an attempt to hand over control of the country to the South Vietnamese while getting our troops out of there. In theory, it sounds like a good idea. In fact, it's a face-saving action to not admit we haven't "won" this war.

Our whole country has been fighting about this war since I can remember. There are the peace-with-honor guys, like my father and my brother Martin, who can face our gradual withdrawal as long as we are training soldiers in South Vietnam, according to the plan you put in place. Then there are the let's-just-get-out-of-there people, who want total withdrawal and no more involvement. This is my mother's and my brother John's stance on it. It's hard to tell what my history teacher's take is on it, since he is always trying to do what he calls the Socratic method with us—that is, he poses an idea, then when we try to line up arguments with the idea, he takes the opposite side. It's annoying.

You did a good thing by signing Title IX into law. My brother John is all about this law because he hopes it means there will be money for me to go to college for athletics. I just started my senior year, so we'll see about that. Your decision-making process here had to be just that it's time for our society to give girls and women the same opportunities as boys and men.

So now you've resigned and are out of office, but we are still in Vietnam. I think it's easier to write to someone who is dead. At least then there is an end to their story. Granted, you inherited Vietnam. Your decision-making process there had to take into account what was already in place. And I think you did well to come up with some way of getting us out of there (it's another letter, or paper, or assignment to figure out what we were doing there in the first place).

You're out of office because of the Watergate scandal and the fact that you probably were going to be impeached. My history teacher, who is the only male schoolteacher I've ever had, is livid about this scandal. It's as if he is personally insulted that you were involved in sneaky behavior. He's particularly incensed that you continue to deny any wrongdoing.

Nobody at my house really cares about Watergate, to tell you the truth. They think all politicians, especially Rockefeller, are crooked. When I try to consider your decision-making process, I think you probably had your own self, your own career in mind, even though you were the president of the United States of America. Like, you were doing everything you could, even if it was illegal, to get reelected. Maybe not all leaders have done illegal things, but if they do, they must suffer the consequences. Our new president has pardoned you. That means, of course, that you won't go to trial or prison for being involved in Watergate. It may not seem fair, but I wouldn't want to be you, leaving the highest office in our land in total disgrace. Sorry, but that's how I feel.

Sincerely,

Claire Joyce

Bishop has a lame intramural team; it's not even organized. Mrs. G., the gym teacher, set up the team, but she doesn't take it all that seriously. It's like an extension of PE. I started playing on the team, but didn't last even two weeks—Mrs. G. does not know how to coach. Period. I truly appreciate Miss Benedict now, who acted like winning and playing were the two most important things of our lives. She doesn't coach Holy Child anymore because she moved to do some work for a college. She already finished college, but she's back at a college, going again. I don't get it.

There's no league to join, either in winter or summer, for girls my age. We just basically try to get pickup games in the schoolyard. Sometimes older girls, who used to play basketball forever in the schoolyard, drop in to play a game. These girls were legends in Holy Child when they were in sixth, seventh, and eighth grades. Then they went to high school, and I don't know what. No more schoolyard. I see it here too. Not just Tina and Diane, but all the other girls— Dorothy, Eileen, Amelia. The game is over for them.

It's not over for me. Why should it be? Not only do the boys have competitive teams in high school, plus Holy Child and CYO, but even the guys who go away to college come back and play in the summer league at the schoolyard. They even have lights at night. If the girls are in the schoolyard, they are there to watch the full-court games. I like watching the games too, but I like playing better.

John scrimmaged a few times in the summer games back after he got out of prison, but he was never part of this schoolyard culture. Before, I loved watching him get in on games. He dribbled fast and low—like, he'd crouch, move slow, then lunge forward past whoever was guarding him. Whoo. Gone. He would fake left, do a complete turnaround, suspend his jump shot in the air, hit the basket.

Sometimes guys that play real good are so full of themselves. I can't stand watching them. John was never like that. He'd do some freakin' magic on a play, then run down the court to get ready for the next play. Those other "star" types either fist pump themselves or talk smack to the other team. Like, "Yeah, that's right, I just did this up in your face," or some taunting thing to get the other team mad. It's ungentlemanly.

So even though I'm deep almost seventeen, I'm still in the schoolyard. The girls are younger than me, but I play pickup games with them. Mostly, though, I play on the half-court by myself, taking shots, dribbling layups, perfecting my foul shot. Diane is at

St. Joseph's College downtown. Tina works at an insurance office on Seventh Avenue, doing clerical stuff, part-time. She's a full-blown girl now. The telltale basketball shadow on her is that her legs are kind of bowed, and she crouches when she walks, so she looks like she's dribbling to me.

John lives in Brooklyn Heights. He's moving up in the Wall Street company so he can afford his place, and still gives money at home. He comes home once a week, gives my mother some money, says hello to me and Bobby, then leaves. I almost feel like writing him a letter to get some conversation with him.

Bobby is getting his GED and working at the phone company. He's still using drugs, bouncing off the walls. The good thing about it is he just comes home and passes out. My mother changed her routine from every other night drinking to sometimes three days in a row, one night off, two days in a row, one night off. My father comes in quietly at 4:00 a.m. and sits in the kitchen, the loneliest person I know besides my mother.

Martin is happy, at least. He and Genevieve and Jake live a few blocks away on the top floor of a brownstone. Genevieve is a really good mother; she hangs around with Jake all day, watching TV, cooking stuff. Sometimes she's still in her nightgown when I drop over after school. She's very content. When Martin comes home, he's usually filthy from the construction work, so he grabs a beer for the shower, then makes the baby laugh hysterically by making funny faces and voices, and running toward him to "get him." I love going over there; it's a happy house.

It's also a relief not to have to explain what I'm doing there. Neither Martin nor Genevieve ever says, "What's going on at home? What time do you have to go? Does Momma know you're here?" They just accept that I'm there and never say anything, except sometimes Genevieve will ask if I'm staying the night. She does it in a flat voice, like saying "Pass the milk." I sometimes start explaining, and both

Martin and Genevieve stop me—like, "What, are you kidding? Stay here. Are you kidding?"

I usually take the ride to school by myself because I'm always a few minutes late. I don't even know why—it's not like I'm putting on makeup or fixing myself up. At Bishop, there are girls who wear mascara and eyeliner, have hairdos, and wear ironed blouses. It doesn't make sense, because we go to an all-girls school. Some of the Puerto Rican girls wear ankle bracelets with their initials and their boyfriends' initials in the hearts. These bracelets are pretty fancy, some even elaborate—two hearts, diamond chips in the middle, wings on the sides, 14-karat gold, pearls creating the circle of the bracelet. Some have jade pearls, some onyx. I know all this because the girls list their ankle bracelets' features, like a car salesman would talk about a car. The girls who wear ankle bracelets have a different kind of walk, a confidence, that comes from having a boyfriend.

Which is the last thing I want. In sophomore year, one of the boys from the schoolyard asked me out. It wasn't to go anywhere; it was just to be his girlfriend. That's what boys do—ask out the girls they want to have as girlfriends. Then the girl acts like that boy is their boyfriend. I was heading home and this boy, John Dixon, ran up to me on the inside of the schoolyard—I was already on the outside—and said through the fence, "Hey, Claire, want to go out with me?" I checked his face to see if he was joking. He wasn't. He looked sincere.

I said, "Okay." Then I kept walking home. I was boyfriended. I had no idea what to do, so I rang Diane's bell and asked her. She told me to call it quits, so I went back to the schoolyard, even though she said to give it a day. I didn't want to be going out with him all night, so I got it over with right away. That was my first boyfriend.

I was relieved then, but now I don't want to be more of a weirdo than I already am—still playing basketball at seventeen, not taking any drugs or smoking pot or drinking (ugh). But not having a boyfriend makes me look suspicious. Meaning, the boys and the girls who I see look like they are sizing me up: is she a lesbian? Like, because I don't act all girly and babyish around boys, I must be either pathetic or a lesbian. I am not a baby at all. I just don't have room to think about a boyfriend, and I'm not thinking about girls, either. I have to think about too many people already. I love coming to Martin and Genevieve's because I don't ever have to think of anything when I'm here.

I babysit mostly for Martin and Genevieve and definitely don't take any money from them. Genevieve's okay with it, but I always have to convince Martin that I really don't want it. Really, I should be giving *them* money—I eat everything they have in the fridge, or any cookies or snacks they have around. Sometimes I leave only one piece of meat in the cold cut pack, or only two Oreos in the pack. They never say anything about it, but they have to notice. Once Jake goes to sleep, I'm reading and eating like it's a party.

I love the quiet. It's so peaceful to be in a house where you can hear the heat coming up, where the sound of the refrigerator humming feels friendly. Maybe, most of all, the sound of a baby sleeping just calms the whole place down. When Martin and Genevieve come home, they always sit in the living room with me for a little bit, watching Johnny Carson or the end of a movie I'm watching. Martin will have a snack, Genevieve will drink water, and I'll finish off a soda. I never have to report what happened during the night; they never ask. It's always the same, anyway. I do my homework, read some books, sometimes just sit and stare. I'll make stuff up sometimes about what I'll do in the future—like, I'll be a detective who solves a big case, or I'll be the first woman to play professional basketball, or maybe I'll go to college. They just let me be there, having a time-out. I love them for that.

REFEREE

"You're not taking the test? What the hell are you thinking?" My mother is screaming at Bobby. I'm in the hallway, coming home from school. I wait for a moment; this sounds serious.

"I'm not taking it, that's all," he says. "The test is moronic, I don't need it to work at the phone company, and it's my business. Mind your own."

"You mind your manners, young man," my mother says. "You take this test and pass it, moronic or not, and you will have a high school diploma!"

"I won't!" screams Bobby. I hear something get thrown, crash down. I run into the kitchen.

"What's going on?" I say, but casual, as if I'm asking, "What time does the movie start?" I have worked on this for such a long time being fake calm is almost natural to me.

"None of your business. Get the hell out of here," Bobby says. He pushes me hard out of the kitchen. I don't resist. Bobby is on high anger now, so anything can happen. I'm worried about my mother. She runs in between us, nudges me toward the hallways, and says, "Go on, Claire. I'm talking to your brother."

I look from him to her and feel my stomach go sour. I won't be budged.

"What's going on?" I repeat.

"What's going on? I'll tell you!" Bobby runs toward me; I brace. He punches me on the side of my head, over my mother.

"No, no, that's enough!" my mother yells. "Please leave, Claire." She is pleading with me. I don't know why, but I make things worse with Bobby. I know it, but I can't help it. It's like my very existence makes him hate.

But how can I leave my mother with him?

"What is wrong with you?" I scream at him. "Quit school, don't take the test to get your equivalency, who cares, just do whatever you're going to do, who cares? Why do you have to be like this to us?"

He lunges past my mother, puts his hands around my neck, squeezes, squeezes . . . I am kicking him, punching him, trying to pull his hands off. My mother is pulling his hands too. She is screaming for him to stop, begging God to do something, asking Jesus to help her. Bobby's face is almost happy looking, it is so crazy. Spittle is coming out of his mouth. His lips are contorted into two broken lines. His eyes are bright and alive with his intention. He is going to kill me.

Then he lets me go, punches me in the head again, and walks out of the house.

My mother pulls me to the nearest chair. I sit, catching my breath, choked anyway. My head is ringing; my body is shaking. Tears run out of my eyes, nose, mouth. My mother is wiping my face with a dish towel, bent over me, sick right to the heart. She keeps saying, "I'm so sorry," over and over. I shake my head no, come to my senses, breathe deeper. It's okay; we're alive.

Neither of us knows what to do about Bobby. He's mental. It's not even a joke.

"O my God, I believe in you. O my God, I adore you. O my God, I hope in you. O my God, I love you."

This is a song the old monsignor at Holy Child wrote. Monsignor was so old, he looked like he wasn't going to make it to the offertory. Every Sunday, at whatever Mass he was assisting, he sang this song that he made up. We all sang it with him. Monsignor's voice was deep, but it trembled with old age and probably all of his faith. When he sang, all the ladies in the church cried. It was like a howl of love from an animal; he choked and barked and moaned the words. The way he sang it almost even made me cry.

God was the only one monsignor loved, though. I mean, he didn't just not like kids. He hated kids. If he came to the schoolyard with his cassock dress with the purple trim and the little Italian hat with the purple pom-pom, I prayed he wouldn't look my way. He threw this look around the schoolyard, at everybody. The look said, "You're all sinners!" He made you feel guilty for nothing.

Once he caught a couple of kids making out under the staircase leading to the boys' section. He grabbed them, smacking them both across their faces. He was old, but he looked like he could do damage.

When we first moved here, I was standing in front of the statues of the crucifixion outside the church. There was Jesus on the cross, already dead, and Mary and another disciple on either side at his feet. I stood there, holding on to the fence, getting sick to my stomach at the sadness of it. I felt Jesus dying as if he were dying that afternoon, like he waited for me to come home from school before he died. I was two breaths short of crying out loud. I felt someone walking behind me, turned around, and saw monsignor. His hands were behind his back, head bent down. I wanted to cry to him, ask him why Jesus had to die, why people are so confusing, how to change the world, why he never smiled. I said, "Father . . ."

Monsignor jerked his head, pinned me with his no-eye stare, and asked me what did I think I was doing. "Go home, girl," he said.

He's dead now. He died over the summer, and the whole parish turned out for his funeral, like they were burying the pope. Everyone said what a holy man he was. Everyone broke down when they sang "O My God."

* *

John lives in a two-bedroom apartment on Henry Street, downtown. He rents it with a friend of his from work. He's had two promotions since he started at Automatic Data Processing. He says brokerage is not the only thing they do; they automatically do the payrolls for a lot of banks and companies in New Jersey and in New York. John works in operations, which means he takes care of the actual movement of a sale or deal from the original "idea" of it to the routing of it through the system. His new title is assistant to the director of risk management, night operations. The company is going to send him for a certificate or something, for risk. He's making good money, my mother says.

He is just himself on weekdays. Starting on Friday night, though, he messes around with something other than drinking. I've seen him on Friday night. He thinks he looks normal. He doesn't.

When he first got the job, my mother gave him the A&S charge card to get "a couple of basics and a suit." He's already paid her back, plus the money he gives to her every week is way more than she is used to getting. John might even make more money than my father, but nobody is saying.

My father leaves money on the table every morning—sometimes it's twelve dollars, sometimes it's twenty dollars. He leaves it under the salt and pepper shakers. That's the money for everything in the house. Martin gives my mother money too, but I don't know how much. Bobby gives her money, even when he's working part-time. Plus, there's John's contribution. So why are we always so poor?

Of everybody, I'm very comfortable with John. He'll still drop by the fence in the schoolyard when I'm playing, ask me about school, answer questions about his job or where he's going. He has a girl-friend whose house he sleeps over at a lot. I can't tell if he likes his job, but I know for a fact that he likes the money he makes. He folds up a wad of it when he gives it to my mother. Then he'll slip me a five or a ten and tell me to invest in the stock market. He probably gives

Bobby money too, but they fight a lot, mostly about how stupid Bobby was for quitting school.

John and even Martin don't know about how Bobby gets crazy and tries to kill me. For sure, my father doesn't know. Only me and my mother know this. That time he threw a glass at me and I had to get stitches, we told the emergency room doctors and clerks that I fell on a broken glass—back of my leg, the fleshy part of my thigh, twelve stitches. The thing is, he felt so bad, he even cried. We felt terrible for him.

And it only kept me out of the schoolyard for a week, but Diane and Tina called for me every day to go to the park. At the end of the summer I went with them, watched them smoke their stupid cigarettes, then some pot. I listened to their ideas about some of the boys they liked, laughed with them about how the stoners from Hippie Hill thought they looked so cool but were really such losers.

Diane and Tina are not losers at all. They don't know that I secretly am. Getting good grades, looking okay, being athletic at basketball feels less and less like who I am. The things I keep inside are who I really am, and they aren't good. Nobody would think so.

PICK AND ROLL

The snow is my favorite weather. I feel holy in the snow, like I'm praying, as it drifts past my window, way up here on the third floor, on its way to the world. I sometimes imagine this is the punished snow, having to fall here instead of some rolling field in Prospect Park, with hundreds of trees to land on softly. Half of the flakes that fall here will be slaughtered by traffic before they can accumulate to protect themselves.

A light snow is falling, so early this year. It feels like I have to start making some definite plans. Every single moment when I'm not in school, or lost in my head, or at the store for my mother, or doing the laundry at the laundromat, or traveling on the bus—I am dribbling, shooting, faking, passing, pivoting, switching, laying up, setting, guarding, running, and most of all, thinking about my game. Most times, I can get Around the World on only two turns. I'm a freak.

I play in the schoolyard every day, still. I'm the oldest girl there. I understand that it might be time to stop playing; I know this because of what is happening around me. Girls have moved on to drinking and smoking in Prospect Park. I'm like the lonely girl in the schoolyard—a big doof, probably a lezzy, like some idiot said. Ha. John Dixon pushed that kid with all his might when he said that. I wasn't even insulted by that kid, but I was happy to see that John Dixon has no hard feelings about me breaking up with him so fast.

I'm good at this. I'm good at basketball.

During the summer, we all go to the band shell on Tuesday and Thursday nights to listen to rock bands. The bands are mostly guys who are just starting out, who cover famous bands, like the Stones or the Beatles or the Rascals. Some of the bands try to cover the Doors or Vanilla Fudge, but they usually sound horrible. To do music like the Doors takes better musicians and definitely better singing. If you don't do Vanilla Fudge with just the right expertise on the electric guitar, it sounds like you're warming up instead of playing.

One Tuesday night, I walk over to the band shell with Tina, Diane, and a couple of the guys they've started to hang around with. They're nice guys, not schoolyard types, more like bowling or baseball types. Still, it's nice to walk through the park with happy guys. One guy came from Carroll Gardens. His name is Michael, and he plays drums in a basement band. He's walking next to me. I tell him I like his shirt. He seems genuinely flattered, which makes me want to laugh.

"Thank you!" he says. "I think my mom got it at Martin's?"

"Oh, yeah, that's a good store," I say. "Well, it's really nice." It's a maroon collarless shirt with three buttons down the front, cotton.

"Do you go downtown shopping?" he asks me.

"Yes, usually to A&S, but not that much. I usually go to the boutiques on Fifth Avenue," I say, which is true, since I bought one pair of jeans in the men's store, Sam's, about a year ago.

He's smiling at me, walking along with me, which is pretty fast, so we're ahead of everyone else. He has dark hair that looks really, really clean, jeans, and that nice shirt. I want to ask him a million questions, but I don't. Casually, I ask him where he goes to school.

"I go to Xavier, in the city?" he says. "Coming up on my last year. How about you?"

I tell him Bishop, coming up on my last year too. I already know he's smart because Xavier boys, the couple I know, are very smart. Plus, John went there for almost two years.

"Are you thinking about college?" he asks me.

I tell him sure, but not sure where yet. I ask him where he's thinking about going.

He nods like he understands exactly what I'm talking about. "I looked at a few schools in the spring with my parents. I have a couple in mind," he says.

"Away?"

"Definitely," he says. "The schools I like are in Michigan and California."

I croak laughing. "Michigan?" I say, like he said Mars. California is not even something I can fool around about.

He laughs too. "That's what my mother thinks. I'm not sure about them, but I liked University of Michigan. They have a great arts and design program, but you don't have to choose a major right away, and their campus is huge—have you looked at any schools?"

"Not really," I say.

"Are you thinking about staying in New York?"

"Really, I'm not thinking about it too much. I figure I'll look into it in the fall when school starts."

"Oh, that's cool," he says, but I think he feels stupid for talking about school, so I tell him I think it's smart to plan ahead.

"It's really my school that gets us started in junior year—no, freshman year!" he says. "They've been talking about college since I got there. A lot of times I wondered if high school was just a pit stop on the way to college—you know what I mean?"

I nod, but I actually don't know what he means. But I like the way he talks.

"Do you play any sports?" I ask, because the truth is, this is what would be the real measure of him.

"I ran track freshman year, but I've been playing rugby for the past two years. I'll be playing this year too," he says.

I do not know what rugby is, but I imagine that it involves horses. I don't say anything but nod like I know what he means.

"How about you? Any sports?" he asks.

"Basketball," I say.

"Oh, cool, does your school have a team?"

"Just an intramural one, but I was on Holy Child for four years. We won the CYO championship two years in a row." I hate that I'm bragging but can't help it.

"That's right!" he says, looking really glad about it. "You played against Mary Star of the Sea, didn't you? That's my parish."

"Yes," I say, totally impressed that he knows this.

"Wow, you must be a good player," he says. I turn to him, to read his meaning. He looks at me expectantly, as though he really wants me to say if I'm good or not.

I laugh, shake my head, ask him if he's a good rugby player. He says, "I'm great." Then he laughs and looks at me to make sure I'm getting his joke. I totally get it. I like him a lot.

When we get to the band shell, it's almost dark. There are fifty or sixty kids listening to a boy band play a slower Stones song. In the middle of the crowd, I see someone with a body-size wooden cross hanging on his back, and two older guys genuflecting and making the sign of the cross in front of him. They're laughing and making fun of the guy. Something inside me seizes up, sends cramps to my heart. The guy wearing the cross turns around. It's John.

He's slack-faced. He's wearing his work shirt, unbuttoned; suit pants; and tie-up leather shoes. He's slowly turning around and around, like a very slow ring-around-the-rosy. The cross is tied around his back. His arms are straight out, as if he were being crucified. His head hangs lower than his neck. The guys around him are laughing, but nobody looks as wasted as he does. I start walking toward him, even though my instinct is to turn back. He's a magnet; I have to see what's happening with my brother. Michael touches my elbow, says something I can't hear because the sound of the amateur band has left me deaf. I can hear only my own breath, moving in and out, loudly.

"Little Miss," John says when he sees me, smiling stupidly.

"What's going on?" I say. I stand between John and one of the guys, Jimmy somebody, who I will hate for the rest of my life because of how he was making fun of John, and I put my hand on the wooden cross that's on John's back. "What is this? What are you doing?"

John can't answer because, based on his unfocused, glazed eyes, he's in another world.

"Take this off," I say, pulling at the cross, but John keeps turning around in a circle. Then he walks away from me, with Jimmy somebody following him, tugging at the cross that's on John's back. Jimmy looks back at me with a stupid apology face that is still laughing. "Okay, we were just fooling around," he says. "It's off, okay?" He's talking to me, untying the rope that held the cross on John's back, but I'm ignoring this idiot.

John's nodding to the music, not even aware I'm standing there. He starts to walk off, toward the Ninth Street park entrance, and I just watch him go without following him. By now, it's dark. The band is loud and awful. The playground behind the bandshell has kids going up and down, back and forth on the big swings, and my eyes are having a hard time adjusting to the shadows. I'm going to cry. I have to get out of there.

I turn and exit back the way I came. I realize, after walking a bit, that Michael is walking next to me, not saying anything. I'm not saying anything, either. We walk all the way to Fifteenth Street, not talking. I don't look at him. I don't say goodbye. I just go home. He comes all the way to the door with me. He doesn't say goodbye or anything. He really is smart.

"I saw John in the park," I tell my mother in the kitchen.

"He was at the band shell?" she asks.

"Somebody that looked like him, that's what I'm saying."

"What are you getting at?" she says. "Stop the nonsense, and say what you're saying."

"He wasn't good—he was on drugs."

My mother stares at me for a moment, shoulders peaked back, like she's ready to go do something. Instead, she says, "All right now. All right," as if she's fully aware of the situation.

I did not tell her because I thought she would immediately do something about it. I told her because I didn't want to be alone with it. She's in the kitchen, not drinking, reading a book. It should be a good night. I don't care. I'm mad at her. I'm mad at my father too. Just because he's never home doesn't mean he shouldn't do something— about everything—too.

But who I'm really mad at is John. I feel a new feeling about him, about his life, about my life too, everything. I'm ashamed. Before, I believed that John could not do anything about what trouble he was in. I didn't care what anybody else thought about him—he was the best guy, the good guy, Mr. Awesome. My friends Tina and Diane would never think to say anything bad to me about John, or Bobby, either. I'd kill them. Whatever reason John had for doing drugs, I just prayed it would pass, and that would be that. He's almost twenty-four; it's taking forever. Now I have the worst feeling I've ever had. I'm ashamed of John.

My mother is always praying for him, for Bobby, probably for all of us, but the ones in trouble always get the most prayers. I wonder if she talks about this in confession? God doesn't seem like an "ever-present help in trouble" like the novena advertises. He seems more like a punisher, an all-seeing omniscient judge who doesn't lift a finger to help anyone out. So even if God does see what's happening with the Joyce family, we have no allies outside of ourselves. We can't just quit and get pardoned. It's our family, our tight little circle. And nobody knows what to do about anything.

DOUBLE VISION

Diane and Tina call for me. They're going to the band shell. I tell them, leaning over the banister as they look up from two flights down, that I'm staying in.

"Come on, Claire, Diane has something important to tell you," Tina says.

"Is everything okay?" I call down.

Diane says, "Yes, but I really do need to talk to you."

Weird. Tina is with her, so it can't be such an emergency.

"Do you want to come up?" I ask.

"No, I have to go over to the band shell because I told my parents I'd be there. You know them—they might drive over to check," Diane says.

This is true. Diane's parents show up and look out their car window, not only at the band shell but at dances, at the soda shop, anywhere. It's like they swear she's lying about where she goes. Diane is so not a liar; you'd think her parents would know that by now.

They're both looking up through the turn in the banister. I can't think up a good fake out not to go. Even my mother has been cajoling me to go out, offering to buy me a Benny's ice or a sundae from Lewnes. It's been only a week, but it's obviously noteworthy I haven't been out.

I spent the whole week reading the next books on the schedule for senior year. Plus, I listened to records, watched TV, and just hung out in the house. This whole week my mother didn't drink, either.

She was reading too, as usual in the kitchen. Bobby would walk in and out, look at my mother, then at me, but he didn't ask any questions. It was quiet; it should have been nice, but it felt sad.

Tina and Diane called for me every day. Even some of the girls in the schoolyard—the younger ones—rang my bell because they were trying to get up a full-court game. I told all of them I couldn't go out. Each time, when I came back in from the hallway, my mother looked at me over her eyeglasses. I gave her a look that said "What?" She let it go.

Part of me is toying with the idea of being done with basketball. Reading *Tess of the d'Urbervilles* makes me feel stupid for all my thinking about and playing basketball. I'm working on losing interest in it. I can't just turn it off, though. It's in me. Even this week, it just feels like an official time-out. Go to school, come back, preserve energy. Time-out.

Tina and Diane are waiting for my answer. It feels like it would take so much energy to get clean jeans on, tie my sneakers, and go all the way downstairs. But I do. I want to see what Diane wants to talk about.

"Hi," I say, as I come down the last flight of stairs.

"Yay, there you are!" Diane says. She puts her arm around my shoulder, gives me a little squeeze.

"What's going on? What's up?" I say.

Tina is smiling at me, looking like she loves me or something.

"What's wrong with *you*?" I ask her.

"Nothing. I missed you! You haven't been out in, like, a year," she says.

"Funny. What's going on, Diane?"

"Let's walk toward the park, okay?" Diane asks. "I'll feel better walking and talking."

We leave my hallway, pass the pizzeria, Holy Child, and get halfway to Lewnes when the three guys we were walking with last week come walking toward us, Michael in the middle. Diane and Tina act all surprised, but you'd have to be an idiot not to know this was planned. Much as I want to run, I stand my ground and act like nothing is out of the ordinary. Even I am amazed at the sheer acting ability I'm exhibiting.

"Hi, girls," says the goofy one, Tina's crush, Georgie Panza. "Where you all going?"

There is general small talk about coming out, going to the band shell, what are you guys doing, want to walk with us? I am half-smiling, half-sick to my stomach because I am following the back-and-forth with a neutral face, but inside I'm cringing.

Michael hasn't said anything about surprises, or hey, funny to meet you here. I look at him, say, "Hi." I give him a little smile because it wasn't his fault my brother stood in the middle of the band shell last week, exploding. He was really nice about it then, but I'm not expecting anything from him.

He says, "Hi. Want to walk over to the band shell with me?"

"Okay, we're all walking there. Let's go."

I was not going to the band shell. I was going only to find out what Diane wanted to talk about. I was going only as far as the park, then going home. I peek at Diane, on the off chance she really does have something she just *needs* to tell me. She has a hopeful, guilty, I'm-sorry-but-it's-cool-right? face on. She is somebody that it's really hard to get mad at, and with that face on, it's impossible. I shake my head a little, give her a one-sided smirk. She knows it's all right, even if I was fooled.

Michael is walking next to me, probably expecting me to walk as fast as I usually walk, but I'm keeping pace with the others. He's asking me about movies and TV shows, which ones I like. He is so unembarrassed about talking to me, without trying to bring the others into the conversation, that I have to admire it a little.

We start naturally walking faster, moving ahead of the others.

He says, "I have something for you," and hands me a Martin's department store bag.

"What's this?"

"It's that shirt you liked—they were on sale, and I asked my mother to get me another one," he says. "I got navy blue. It'll look nice with your eyes."

"You got me a shirt?"

"Yeah, it's no big deal, but you liked it, and I figured I'd get it for you."

"I don't even . . . What . . . You're crazy, this is really nice."

"Take it out, look at it. I think it'll fit you. I got you a medium."

He looks like he's so concerned that I might not like it, or that it might not fit.

"I love it, are you kidding?" I say. "This is so really, really nice. I can't even believe it." I am wearing a gray T-shirt that has been washed five hundred times, at least. This blue shirt looks like the most beautiful shirt I've ever seen. "I'm going home to put it on," I say.

Michael smiles with his whole face. "I'll walk you."

Not many people know this, but I am a total lover of all presents. Something like this happened before to me. My friend from St. A's, Maureen Quirk, was wearing a really cool American sweater—the one that's white with cranberry and blue stripes by the V-neck—and I told her how much I liked it and how cool it was. On my birthday, she gave me a box with a brand-new American sweater in it. I will never forget that.

Michael walks me back to my house, through the park, talking about his drums, his band, college, and asking me about all my plans, what things I like. He doesn't say one word about last week. When we get to my house, I tell him I'll be right down. He says, "Sure," and waits by the door.

I tell my mother I'm home to change into a shirt someone gave me and leave it at that. She starts asking all kinds of questions, but I am somebody who doesn't have to answer all her inquiries now. In the bathroom, I wash my face, find some lip gloss in the medicine cabinet, put some on. Michael's right; the shirt looks nice with my eyes.

BANK SHOT

I haven't been paying attention to my mother lately, or worrying about Bobby or John. I still go to Martin and Genevieve's to see my amazing nephew, Jake, but I'm not there all that much, either. A couple of times that I've noticed, my mother puts on her coat after dinner and goes out. She always says she's "meeting some people she knows." Good for her, but I don't care what she does, or what anybody else does. I'm a senior.

And I have a boyfriend who is nicer than anybody. Michael is all about college right now. He makes it seem like it's an achievable goal for me. I make an appointment just before Thanksgiving to meet with the guidance counselor at Bishop to float the idea.

Mrs. Fitz is short, big legged, and sarcastic. She starts out our meeting by saying, "Well, this is the first time I've seen you. Did you just wake up?"

I tell her I didn't think college was an option, but now I'd like to explore the idea. Could she help me? In my mind, I am shooting a basketball against the white backboard, *bang, bang,* just to watch the pole shake. Mrs. Fitz seems attentive to my direct eye contact, and I imagine she can feel how solidly I'm lobbing these questions.

"Oh, yes, I see you have excellent grades," she says, looking at my transcripts, surprised. "Seriously, Claire, why haven't you come to see me before this? There's very little time now, if you're thinking of a scholarship."

I back dribble, saying something about money, options, work, and how I'm not even sure I can afford it, but I'd like to know what's possible.

"Don't worry about affording it. City College has open admissions, and you'll certainly be able to get into Brooklyn College or even Hunter College," she says. "I'm thinking Marymount Tarrytown, too. Were you thinking about going away to school?"

I nod, free throw. "What is the possibility of going somewhere where they have a girls' basketball team?" I ask. Michael is currently fixated on a school in Connecticut that has a great rugby team. He doesn't expect a scholarship; he doesn't ever say he needs one.

"Girls' basketball?" Mrs. Fitz laughs. "That's a long shot, pardon the pun." She is overly pleased with her joke. Clearly, she didn't plan it, it just slipped out, but she is taking conscious credit for it.

I am not smiling. It's her turn: take the ball out, Mrs. Fitz.

"Well, of course, there are college teams, but I honestly don't know much about them. I guess you really like basketball?"

Dead ball.

"Okay, thanks. Can I apply for City College or Brooklyn College? They're open admissions?"

"Yes, dear. I'll give you the paperwork, you fill it out, then return it to me. We'll take care of sending your records—you really do have very good grades—but you must move fast," she says. "No interest in Marymount?"

"Could I get a scholarship?" I ask.

"Maybe. Have you taken the SATs? Good scores on that, together with your record, could get you a small scholarship, I'm sure," she says.

"Yes, I'll take the next SAT, but I need more than a small scholarship," I say. "City College is free, so that's probably a better option."

She gives me the date for the SAT—next Saturday. I ask her to sign me up. I need more guidance than I'm getting from Mrs. Fitz, but I'm not sure who to ask. Bishop has a unique twist on girls' Catholic high schools, because its faculty consists of four different orders of nuns: St. Joseph, Dominican, Sisters of Charity, and Sisters of Mercy. Each of the different orders is in charge of certain subjects. The sisters of St. Joseph teach religion and English—they're usually nuns who look overly preoccupied and stern. Dominicans teach math, science, and history—they're nuns who look like they run businesses, because they're crisp and clear. Charity nuns teach home ec (cooking, sewing, family living)—they look like they barely passed their own high school courses but are on a mission to tidy up. The Sisters of Mercy do all the administrative work in the school, like the office, detention, and nurse's station. Laypeople teach gym, usually women who ref over the weekends at CYO games. These are the brutes of Bishop— no mercy, no fooling around, get moving is their collective attitude. There is no palling around with teachers here. We go to class, do our work, and that's that.

The nicest teachers are the Dominicans because they like to joke around a little. One of the nicest nuns is Sister Joan Harding, who uses her real name instead of a saint's. Sister Joan seems like she gets that there's a world out there, more than any nun I've ever met. I've been taught by nuns for twelve years, so I know some things about them.

For one thing, nuns get incredibly embarrassed if they're wrong about something. They can really lose their cool, either turning red or stammering, or getting so mad that they take it out by giving extra homework. But not Sister Joan. She was asked, respectfully, about an answer in math class that she posted on the board. The answer was wrong, and the very brave and smart Monse Olivero pointed it out to her. I knew it was wrong too, as I'm sure half the class did, but we either didn't care, or we figured it wasn't worth the effort to watch Sister Joan squirm for being wrong.

She surprised us by laughing at her mistake, erasing it, and telling Monse Olivero that she was the teacher today. The only way to describe it: she was just nice. Not just *acting* nice, but to-the-bone nice. We all kind of loved her.

The other thing about nuns is that the real situations and problems of their students scare them. They don't want to hear it. In freshman year, Julia Biancini got in trouble for crying. She was sitting in homeroom, talking to her friends who sat in front of and next to her (I was across the aisle, behind her). She was telling them very personal stuff about her father moving out and her mother sleeping all day, when Sister St. Hugh, the St. Joseph religion and homeroom teacher, sent her to the dean. She told the girls in the class to concentrate on the day ahead, or we'd all get demerits. So basically, if the world entered the classroom in any way, we'd get in trouble.

Sister Joan wasn't like that. She was kind. One time, a very nervous girl, Miranda Gonzalez, was fidgeting during an exam, and Sister Joan walked over to her desk with a piece of paper. She put the paper on Miranda's desk and folded it over and over, creating a flower. She didn't say one word to Miranda; she just leaned over her desk, folding up a calm flower. It was very relaxing; I was watching her, feeling mesmerized by what she was doing. I'm sure Miranda Gonzalez felt the same way.

I decide to ask Sister Joan if she knows anything about basketball in college. I just have to find the right time.

John is in the kitchen when I get home. He looks normal.

"Hey, Little Miss—wait, Big Miss! Hold on, stand up, what? You're Too Tall. That's your new name," he says. He's standing next to me, and I don't have to look up to look him right in the eye. I'm five feet nine inches.

"What are you doing here?" I ask. It doesn't come out right—I mean to say, how are you, what's new, what's going on, haven't seen you in so long, how's your apartment, your job, your drug life? He's totally cool with it, in any case.

"I stopped in to see you guys," he says.

I'm looking at him, and at my mother, and I'm silently sniffing the air to see if anything's wrong. Doesn't seem to be. My mother sits at the kitchen table, looking up at me so expectantly, as she does lately. Like she's waiting for me to say something of utmost importance. I don't get her anymore. I don't even try. I'm just thinking about myself.

"Good to see you." I give him a smile, turn around to drop my books and sneakers, and head to my room.

"Claire, where are you going?" John asks. "Stay here and talk a minute."

"What? I'm going out tonight, and I have to get this work done before I go," I say.

I don't want to stay and talk; I don't want to listen. I don't care. I hate the part of me that is ashamed of him, which makes me hate him too. They don't know that I am doing everything I can to leave this house, to leave them all. Mrs. Fitz informed me that I could most assuredly get money and a work-study job at Marymount, should I decide on that school. I'm not crazy about going to Marymount, because a few St. Saviour girls I know go there and they're total lames—smart but uncoordinated.

From my room, I hear the murmur of talking between my mother and John. Bobby is still working at some maintenance company where he cleans offices every single night, and still refusing to take the GED. It's so stupid I can't even talk about it. He gives my mother money, comes home sometimes around the same time as my father, and I have nothing to do with any of them. I still feel a little sorry for my mother, but I don't let myself think about it.

John knocks at the door to the front room, where I'm sitting on my bed, looking at which book to begin first.

"Nice, knocking on the door," I say. Nobody does that; it's kind of funny.

"Hey, I feel like I haven't seen you in months, Claire," he says. "I know you're in school and playing intramurals, Momma said. I hear you have a boyfriend?" He tries to say this with a straight face, but he can't help smiling after he says it.

"Duh. Big deal," I say.

"No, that's great, really," he says. "Does he live around here?"

"No."

"He's a senior, too?"

"Yup."

"Nice, cool, good." At each word, he waits a beat for me to fill in the space with information. I am writing my heading on the loose-leaf.

"Doing any ball in the schoolyard?" he asks.

I stop to look at him, breathe out through my nose. Like, does he realize I'm seventeen? The schoolyard is for quick pickup games, not for hanging out anymore—even for me.

"Thinking about college?" he wants to know. So that's what this is about, I figure. He's got a thing for that, always. I wish I felt more like talking to him. But I don't.

"Little bit, probably City College. I'll let you know when I know," I say.

"Little Miss, you are being inscrutable."

I roll my eyes like, get over that name already.

"You know I'm going to help you out with college, right?"

"What? No, you don't have to, thanks," I say. I actually want to kill him for being nice right now. He should just leave, because I'm acting really rude to him. Doesn't he get it?

"Listen to me. Hey, listen," he says.

I look up at him.

"It's a good thing," he says, "you going to college. I'm going to help. I want to help, so look around where you want to go. Don't just take the first thing."

"You take drugs," I say. I'm breathing roughly.

He lowers his eyes, then nods. "You're right. I have taken drugs," he says. "But I'm not addicted, and I don't take them on a regular basis."

"What does that mean?"

"It means that I don't take drugs to the point of addiction and that I use them recreationally. You don't have to worry about that, Claire."

"I'm not worried about it," I say. "You should be worried about it."

He laughs. "I will, if it gets to the point where I should be."

I look back at my loose-leaf, shake my head, look back up at him, still shaking my head.

"Go back to work," he says. "I have to leave, but we're definitely talking about college again, soon."

"Take care," I snort.

"Apply to different colleges," he says. He points his finger at me as he walks backward out the door.

THREE POINTER

I'm not one of those girls who has a boyfriend and that's the end of her life. I really like Michael; he's smart and he pays attention. He is a good kisser, not that I would know the difference. But if someone is kissing you, and you're all tingly and breathy, they must be a good kisser. I could definitely do more than kiss.

We see each other mostly on weekends, though sometimes we meet up on Thursday nights in the Village. His school is on Sixteenth Street, so it's an easy ride on the F train to West Fourth Street. I meet him by Washington Square Park, which is also the "campus" of New York University, though you'd never know it. NYU has all the buildings around the park, but the park is for everyone. I swear, you can get high just walking there—that's how much it reeks of pot. Plus, there's so many people selling drugs of all kinds there, hanging out almost like it was a drug shopping center. At the same time, there are all kinds of hippies throwing Frisbees, playing guitar, wearing no shoes. It's like the Easter Sunday Central Park Be-In, except it's every day in Washington Square Park.

We're not hippies, but we don't mind them. They're usually stoned, so the worst thing they do is talk to you in a smiley, wacky way. Michael and I walk through the park around five, but I get to the city at four so I can hang out on Sixth Avenue and West Fourth, watching the pickup games in the schoolyard. This is serious basketball. The guys who play here are either trying to go pro, or they played college ball and now this is their only type of competition. It's the best basketball around. But it's dirty. Fouling, left and right. Guys skidding on their knees across the concrete, then getting back up to play with the blood running down their legs. Jammed fingers, which hurts so much, being pulled out by teammates and, unbelievably, the guys not even letting out a whoop. No refs, no time-outs, just playing until the score is twenty-one. You have to be good to play here, no question.

Sometimes Michael will meet me there, but he's not really a basketball guy. He appreciates it, but it doesn't thrill him the way it does me. Sometimes when I'm sitting in class, I like thinking of these guys. I imagine that someone is on the court on Sixth Avenue, dropping points, crazy-magic dribbling, stealing the ball and a shot. It always makes me smile.

We're walking through Washington Square Park, and Michael tells me he has a surprise. He holds up two tickets to the Knicks vs. Celtics, tomorrow night.

"Oh my God," I say. "What? How? Oh my God." I have never been to a Knicks game or to Madison Square Garden.

"My uncle got the tickets from his partner, court seats," Michael says.

"Holy shit!" I yell. "No, really, holy shit."

I cannot believe I am going to see Bill Bradley, Walt Frazier, Earl the Pearl, and Phil Jackson, *live*!

"When will we get there? I'll meet you, right? What time?" I ask.

"We'll meet after school, get pizza, go to the game early," Michael says. "Figure we can get to the Garden at around six. The game starts at eight, so plenty of time." He's excited too.

"This is the best thing that ever happened to me," I say. I don't really think so, but it's close, so I say it.

Michael laughs, says, "Me too," but he probably doesn't think so, either. It's just fun to say.

＊ ＊

My mother is sitting in the kitchen with a churchy-looking woman when I get home. "Claire, this is Isabel," she says.

No last name? My mother always makes us refer to other adults as Mr. or Mrs. "Hi," I say, shaking her hand.

"It's so nice to finally meet you," Isabel says. "I've heard so much about you."

"Thanks," I say, realizing I've heard nothing about her.

"What's going on?" I ask my mother.

"Isabel and I were just reading this book, but we're finished for today," she says, putting a book in her pocketbook.

"Nice," I say. "Good to have met you. Take care." I'm heading into the bedroom to get the whole weekend's worth of homework out of the way. I'm actually dying to tell my mother that I'll be going to Madison Square Garden to see the Knicks play. Her church-lady friend sounds like she's leaving.

These days I know something is different about my mother, but I am in a zone that works for me, so I'm not going to investigate. When I speak with her, it's always about me now. I've heard enough of her to last me.

She comes into my room, tells me that her friend left. I nod without looking at her. I can see her face, though, as if I was looking. She's got that ask-me-about-it face on—hovering around, ready to say something but waiting to be prodded, eyes filled with information.

"I'm going to the Knicks game tomorrow night," I say.

"Oh. That's good!" she says. "Who with? Michael? Did he buy tickets? Will you go on the subway? Of course you will, but what time will the game be over? Will he come back with you to take you home?"

"Yes to all of the questions," I say. "I'll leave from school, put my uniform in my locker, change in the bathroom. Meet Michael by Xavier, walk up to the Garden. We're going to have pizza for dinner. I can't wait." I have busted through a little bit here—this is so exciting!—and my mother is trying to smile and wipe the worry off her face.

"That sounds like a lot of fun, especially seeing the Knicks," she says. "Right up your alley!"

I am waiting for the usual douse of cold water she throws on any hint of too much happiness; if there's a flaw in a plan, she'll find it. I'm ready for her.

"I just did the laundry, so you'll have clean clothes," she says. "Do you need a bag to bring your change of clothes in?"

"No, I'll use my old gym bag, thanks," I say. She's walking toward the hallway; I look after her. She'll probably say something later, and if she drinks, she will definitely have something nasty to say. She can make the nicest situation seem like you're being taken advantage of, or you are in for a disappointment.

Try as I might not to be, I am very influenced by what she says. I hate that about myself. I've heard so many negative, hateful, awful comments come out of her mouth in that kitchen, beer in hand, that she feels like a walking car accident. She always tried to make up for her meanness by being her "nice" self the next day—a little nervous, interested in you, concerned about how everyone is doing, smart about reading and movies, even wise about life. But her tirades and drunkenness left such a bad feeling, it got harder and harder to forgive her. When I look at her life, I don't think it's so bad. Now I am finished feeling sorry for her.

I'm sitting in the cubby one night, half-watching a stupid show, when Bobby walks in with really great news. He passed his GED, which he didn't tell us he was taking, and he's enrolling at Brooklyn College for the spring session! That's in, like, three months! I'm seriously happy for him, and he even looks less mental. He really used to be sweet and gentle, if a little slower than the rest of us. Not intellectually, but in his ability to "get" what was going on around him. Like, it takes him longer to process things. There are some girls in my high school like that too.

I've been writing a paper for AP English about the themes and character development in *I Never Promised You a Rose Garden*. I am appreciating, now, how people have different ways of being in the world. It's not about how smart they are, or how athletic, or if they have mental problems. I can see how people have to build their world out of what their inherent strengths or weaknesses are. It's like we're given building blocks to construct our lives, and we are actually the architects of what we construct. Bobby has to build his world more slowly than maybe everyone else in this family. Maybe my father does too. That's why he is so overwhelmed. It's all going too fast for him.

I tell Bobby how happy I am that he's going to keep going to school, since in reality, he got the best grades of any of us. My mother always says that. Lately Bobby is never around, or if he is, he is high. I think he may have smoked a little tonight, but it doesn't seem like he's taken any other drugs. Otherwise, he wouldn't be sitting here, talking to me. And even though I know Bobby can be a ticking time bomb, I can't help myself. I have to ask him why he didn't just finish his senior year at Bishops.

"I really, really hated that school, and I really, really hated every one of my teachers," he says. "You have no idea how shitty they were to me."

"Why?"

"You know what they told me? The fucking guidance counselor told me I was going to end up in prison, just like my brother."

My mouth is open, and every curse word I know is waiting there, but I can't even speak. I just look at Bobby, who I know that must have hurt so much and for a long time.

"Did you tell Momma?" I ask.

He gives me a how-stupid-are-you face. "No way."

I nod, but then I think, he should have told her. She should have defended him, yelled at them, written a letter to the diocese. But no, I understand. I know exactly what Bobby was doing. He was saving her from the shame she would have felt. We didn't ever want her to feel worse than she already did. So Bobby just took that by himself.

"You should have told me," I say, already fantasizing a variety of revenge plots.

"Why? So you could go over there and bounce your basketball at them?" he says. "'Hey, Father Shithead, catch this friggin' ball,' then you'd throw it at him, hit him in the head, let it bounce back to you, hit him again, two points!"

"I'd hook the shot, hard, right into the middle of his nose, and break it," I say. "Off the rim, for Claire Joyce, in the final quarter of the playoffs, for Holy Child against Wholly Bastards!"

Bobby's laughing. I love that I can still make him laugh.

DUNKING

The greatest thing about the greatest night watching the greatest team in the whole basketball world play basketball against the next greatest team is dunking.

Court seats are magical. Michael's uncle's friend must be rich, because his seats are four rows up from the back of the basket. It's a long view of the game, but we didn't miss anything. There they were—right in front of our eyes, enough to hear their sneakers squeak and the grunting of wrestling down the rebound, seeing their sweat go into their eyes. Who they are on TV is exactly like who they are live. But the dimension is everything. Walt Frazier sways, like a dancer. Bill Bradley's eyes never stop moving; neither does his head, like his mind is always calculating something. Earl the Pearl is so fast and, incredibly, so much taller than he looks on TV. Players I didn't even think much of, like Phil Jackson, are like magicians in person.

The ball looks like a yo-yo in their big hands. They pull it, push it, switch it, cross over, with sleight-of-hand skill. It takes our breath away.

At one point, I am holding Michael's hand in a death grip—I'm afraid I have dreamed myself here. Good sport that he is, he's taking it without complaining.

I keep that grip on his hand until—in the second half, with the Knicks scoring on our side of the floor—dunking happens, over and over. This is the realest thing anyone will ever see, I swear. Up goes The Pearl, alongside the basket, with the pass from Bradley, and he hangs there—*hangs there, midair*—then drops that ball right in the hoop. Untouchable. Defying gravity. In person, it stirs my whole soul. It's terrifying and charming and looks like a ballet. There should be music accompanying it. This is what grace looks like.

I have stood up and am told to sit down by the people behind me. Michael takes my arm and pulls me down. I can't stop looking at the court, and I can't talk to him about any of it right now—or ever. My head feels smacked between two opposites: ferociousness and utter delicacy. These men, these athletic men, are not just playing basketball. They are like great big whales in the ocean, diving for the pure joy of it, coming up and spraying water out their blowholes, then twirling back down.

I love them with all my heart.

FULL=COURT PRESS

Sister Joan is, like, *honored* that I ask her about college. I knock on her third-floor classroom just before afternoon homeroom. When I come in, she has this big smile—what my mother would call a grand smile—and says how happy she is to see me. I get right to it, asking her if she knows about any colleges that might have girls' basketball. She flips out.

"Claire, there's a college in Pennsylvania that has a wonderful girls' basketball team," she says. "Do you know about Immaculata? We were talking about them last night! What serendipity. How are your grades? Still good?"

"Nineties all around," I said. "I'm waiting for my SAT scores."

"Well, I only know a little bit about the school, truly only what I've heard from the other sisters, but let me look into it," she says. "And I will find out about other colleges too. I know Vassar has a team, and I'm fairly certain there are teams at all the women's colleges now. How about scholarship money? We can look into academic scholarships as well. We may even get money for sports." Sister Joan has run away with the ball. Dominican sisters don't fool around. She is hepped up.

"Do you think I have a chance to get into one of those schools?" I ask.

"I see no reason why not, Claire," she says, and she means it.

"I haven't played on a team in more than three years," I tell her. "Intramurals are not really teams, but I practice all the time. Still, I don't have a current record of points per game, or turnovers, or really any record right now."

"Let's cross that bridge when we come to it, and don't worry about what we don't know about," she says. "I'll find out what I can. Come back tomorrow, before afternoon homeroom."

The next morning, in homeroom, a student comes in with a note for my teacher. Sister Miriam, a St. Josephite, not one to mess with and not happy to be saying this, tells me Sister Joan would like to see me, so I should wait until she takes attendance, then go. I nod, pretending I am perplexed and worried, so Sister Miriam will take relief in my suffering. Meanwhile, I just know that Sister Joan wants to tell me something and can't personally wait for the afternoon.

As soon as I walk into her classroom, Sister Joan asks me if it is possible for me to go to Malvern, Pennsylvania, to meet with the coach of Immaculata College. She is practically shaking with excitement when she asks, "Are you really good at basketball?"

I tell her the truth: I know what I'm doing, and I know that I'm solid. I stop myself from telling her I'm not a star, and I don't mention that I know that I'm not because I can recognize stars when I see them play. I run my quick background: MVP, CYO championship, captain of the team. Inside, I'm asking myself the same question she asked me: am I really good at basketball?

But going to Pennsylvania is not going to work. "Do I have to go down there? Can I just write a letter, or get my old coach to write the coach a letter?"

Sister Joan dismisses my worry. "I'm sure that will be just fine, Claire. Do not worry about this at all. If you're interested, I will be happy to make the introductions for you. And please listen to me: this is not the only school with girls' basketball. I have a couple of names of wonderful schools that we will immediately contact for you. Here's the list."

She gives me a notepaper with her handwriting all over it; Sister

Joan has been following up like mad. She's written: Wellesley, Vassar, Bryn Mawr, North Carolina State University, Wayland Baptist, Immaculata.

"They're not in order, dear," she says. "These are names some of the sisters came up with last night. They are certain each of these schools has a basketball team for you."

"Wayland Baptist?" I am agog.

"Actually, that one is in Texas, and I don't know all the details, but Sister St. Hugh says they have a team with a very rich benefactor who makes sure all the girls have everything they need," she says. "We'll find out much more about it. Don't worry about anything. We will help you."

When she says "we," she is not talking about Bishop High School. She is talking about the whole Dominican order of nuns where she comes from. I have no idea where she even lives, but the Dominicans show up together at school and leave together at the end of the day. These math and science teachers mean business.

MOVING VIOLATION

My father sits across from my mother in the kitchen. It's Tuesday afternoon, four thirty; he should be gone. I drop my stuff in the cubby, walk to the archway, and say, "Hi."

He says hi back, then coughs into his handkerchief for almost five minutes straight. I look to my mother, who has refreshed his glass of water, standing there like she is ready to perform CPR. He's not choking on anything. He's just coughing his head off.

It's so rare to see them in the same room that I am embarrassed for them. We have heard the ranting of my mother about my father's lack of ambition, money, involvement, love, intelligence, wit, family loyalty—so often that it's hard for me to imagine why he is still here. Then it occurs to me—he didn't hear these rantings. We did. He was gone at work, then sleeping, then gone again. I hardly know him.

"Are you sick, Daddy?" I ask him, when he settles down.

"No, I'm fine, just a little cough," he says, which starts the coughing again. It's a hacking cough, dry. I instinctively pat him on the back. He looks up at me and smiles through his teary-eyed, red-faced, coughing-choking. I feel deeply sorry for him.

"Want a cup of tea?" I ask.

He shakes his head, coughs out a no, sips water, and works vehemently to settle himself down.

"He needs to see a doctor," I say to my mother. Somehow, it comes out like a dare. Like, "I dare you to do something good for him."

"You're right, Claire, he does. I'm waiting for Dr. Greenstone's evening hours before we leave. He starts tonight at five thirty," she says. She turns to my father. "We'll take the bus down there, Jack, or do you think we should take a taxi?"

"Why don't you call Martin and ask him for a lift?" I say, picking up the phone.

"Yes, yes, good idea," she says. "Give me the telephone. I'll call him."

My father is coughing the whole time we are talking. Martin says he will come right over, and Genevieve wants to know if she can do anything, or if I want to go over to their house. I tell my mother I'll wait here, do my homework, and see them when they come back. She can call me if she needs me to do anything.

Martin comes in, casually pulls my hair, gives my mother a kiss, and bends to look at my father, who is getting smaller and smaller on the kitchen chair. "Come on, old man, let's get you to the doctor," Martin says, not unkindly, but not all that gently, either. He's clearly had a few drinks, but he's not drunk. He starts walking toward the hallway as my mother and I help my father out of the chair.

"Martin!" I yell to him. He turns around, surprised at the level of assistance our father needs. He comes back, takes him under his shoulders, wrapping his strong construction arm completely around him. He easily navigates my father out the door. My mother follows, emptying her purse of papers, books, church bulletins. She hands them to me. I put them down on the kitchen table.

When they leave, I wonder if I should contact John, or even Bobby. Probably not, even though both of their work numbers are in the address book, in case of emergency. This isn't an emergency.

I see the book sticking out of the papers my mother emptied from her purse; it's blue, with blue embossed letters that are hard to read on the cover: *Alcoholics Anonymous*. Now what?

* *

When they come back two hours later, I learn that my father has emphysema. All his smoking, driving a cab, inhaling fumes of car exhausts for the past thirty years has destroyed his lungs. In this order, this is what has to happen: he has to breathe out while pursing his lips so he can fill up his lungs before taking the next breath; he needs to take drugs called steroids; he has to use an inhaler and an oxygen tank; he cannot talk if he is short of breath, ever; and we have to move because he will not be able to climb the two flights of stairs to the apartment.

My brothers plan to chip in twenty dollars more a week each to cover any cost for medicine. Bobby is giving the same amount as Martin and John because he makes full-time money.

I am the only one not contributing. Enough's enough. I vow to get a job downtown as a cashier or a salesgirl in one of the department stores. Lots of seniors at Bishop have part-time jobs. I have gotten away with murder for not working until now—forget the stupid babysitting jobs, which don't pay anything anyway. That's basically Sunday money. I tell my mother I'll be going downtown after school tomorrow to apply for a job. She nods, tells me to do what I think I should do.

I realize that since meeting Michael, I haven't really been a part of my family. Michael wants me to come to his house, a brownstone in Cobble Hill, to meet his mother and father. I always come up with some reason why I can't. If I meet his parents, then he will expect to meet mine. He already knows Bobby from around, and he knows that John is my brother, but I haven't introduced them. I just want to keep it all separate.

My mother starts looking in the neighborhood for an apartment, but it has to have the same rent we have now. All the rents are more expensive than ever. Even the Italian lady who is the landlord here doesn't have any available apartments in her building that we can afford.

But soon enough, she comes home with good news.

"I found a very reasonable apartment on the first floor on Sixteenth Street, between Eighth and Ninth," she says. "Three bedrooms. The rent is two hundred dollars a month, because we will be the supers!"

Bobby says, "I'm already a super." He means he cleans offices.

"What does that mean?" I ask my mother.

"It means that once a week, we will sweep and mop the hallway floors, and two times a week, we'll put out the garbage pails for the sanitation pickup," she says. "It's not bad!"

My father is breathing out through his pursed lips. He looks big-eyed, helpless.

"How many floors?" I ask.

"There are four floors, two apartments a floor," my mother says. "I have it all worked out—Claire, you're looking for a job, right? Well, you can stop because you just got one. You'll do the sweeping and the mopping. Bobby, you'll put the pails out, and I'll take them when they're emptied. Of course, I'll help you too, Claire."

I look over at Bobby, who is nodding, like it's no big deal. I stand a full seven inches taller than my mother, looking down at her. "Why don't you sweep and mop the floors?" I ask.

The way I figure it, my mother has sat home while all of us have gone out to work, school, work, athletics, work, school, everything, always. When does she take a turn?

"I told you, I will help you, miss," she says. "And I will handle any problems that come up in the building, or with the tenants." She is looking straight at me with her what-else-do-you-have-to-say face on.

"Is that in between your nightly meetings to talk about alcohol?" I say.

Now she's pissed. "That is none of your business, and I won't have you besmirching it or my activities. Do you hear me? You keep your attitude and your opinions to yourself from now on—make no mistake about how they're of no interest to anyone here."

She's been "good Mom" for weeks now, calm and interested, going about her business, sneaking off to the Holy Child basement and who knows where else, taking some kind of drinker's cure. Bobby and I haven't spoken, but we're both waiting for the beer cans to show up in the fridge and for the real "Eve" to reappear.

"Go ahead!" I yell. "It's been a while since you were a screaming banshee. Let's hear it. Tell us all off and about how terrible your life's been. Make sure you remind us what a great childhood you had! Wait, you can't? No beer, no screaming? We're all supposed to be so grateful for the peace and quiet. We'll be so happy to mop floors and sweep! We'll make sure to keep tiptoeing around you in case you get upset about something. Don't worry, we're all here to serve you."

Bobby is pushing me, saying shut up; my father is coughing my name. My mother is standing erect, still in her coat, staring at me. She has no anger on her face. She looks just like I want her to look: ashamed.

I grab my coat and walk out. Outside, the sash of Christmas lights strung across the avenue to dress things up for Christmas looks pathetic. They put lights up on three blocks and by Holy Child, but they must have had only one strand left, so they put them up on this side of the avenue, between my house and the delicatessen across the street. They should have done either the whole block or nothing; you can't put up one stupid light strand for a whole block.

I walk over to Sixteenth Street between Eighth and Ninth. My mother didn't give us the address, so I walk down the block trying to imagine which one of the exactly alike apartment houses is the one she's got us all working in. I'm also wondering who lives on this block—there are a couple of girls I know and, for sure, a couple of boys Bobby knows. But they're kind of poor kids, too, so that's not a problem.

I don't even know what the problem is. I get to the end of the block, turn right on Eighth Avenue, and keep walking. I walk and walk; it's not that cold, even though I still have my school uniform and knee socks on. As I walk, I calm down. I pass St. Saviour Church and reflexively look up the block at the high school. It's just one small brick building, but the girls who go there are smart, and most of them go to college. After Third Street, Eighth Avenue starts to look really pretty because the brownstones and limestones are in great shape. It seems like each bay window has a huge Christmas tree in it, the double entry doors have wreaths so fresh I can smell them from the sidewalk, and some of the houses have gaslight lanterns lit up in the areaway, some with fresh greens and red bows. It's beautiful.

At President Street, I turn right and head toward the parkside. This whole block is row after row of brownstones with high stoops, gated areaways, neat garbage cans. It's dark now, past dinner. Prospect Park up ahead looks like a lush forest. It's contained by a low stone wall that continues straight from Grand Army Plaza right up to Fifteenth Street and Bartel-Pritchard Square. How many years I spent walking that wall, on my way from the library and back. Even now, I'm tempted to do it, but I know what it feels like. It's a little-kid thrill.

As much as I love this neighborhood, rich and poor, the park, the schoolyards, the sloping streets, I yearn to leave it. I want to go away to college; I know that now. Nobody is encouraging me to do that, or holding out that idea—except Sister Joan, who should know better. And Michael, who doesn't know any better. John might, but he is like a ghost who slips in and out of the house to give my mother money once a week. Martin and Genevieve both sighed and gave me one-sided smiles when I mentioned I might be looking at some schools for a possible scholarship. It's not so much a fantasy as an idea that is so far-fetched. Even though I know of lots of girls—okay, *some* girls—who went to college, the truth is, I really don't personally know anybody who went away. It's like an idea for somebody else's life.

Passing Fifth Street, I realize that I acted incredibly mean and stupid to my mother. I did what she did, without the beer. I raged. It felt like I was getting rid of bad feelings, blaming her, shoving all the negative thoughts away from me and onto her. I saw my mother and father and Bobby standing there, but I didn't hear them or see them, really. All I heard was my own noise.

It's not her fault that she has to make us be the supers with her; it's not my father's fault that he can hardly breathe. So big deal—I have to sweep and mop once a week. God, I am a spoiled brat. How did I end up like this? *Hail Mary, full of grace, the Lord is with thee, blessed art thou among women and blessed is the fruit of thy womb, Jesus. Holy Mary, Mother of God, pray for us sinners, now and at the hour of our death.* I walk fast toward home, ready to admit I was out of my head and to apologize. *Through Christ our Lord, Amen.*

3=2 ZONE

A week later, we're in the Methodist Hospital, waiting to take my father home from the emergency room. Martin and my mother are in the room, John and I are outside, and Bobby is working. My father started choking so hard tonight he looked like he was going to die. Genevieve called around to bars looking for Martin, but my mother got John on the first try. When Martin arrived at our house, he practically carried my father down the stairs. We all got in the car together, and John pulled up right behind us.

After they've been in there a while, my mother comes out to tell us that our father is being given IV steroids and oxygen. She says the doctor also gave him a needle full of antibiotics and that he might have pneumonia. He really did almost die. But they aren't keeping him overnight, because he'll be more comfortable at home, the nurse told my mother. My mother goes back in, telling us to wait so John can help Martin carry our father back up the stairs. We're moving right after Christmas.

John gets us some candy from the vending machine, and we sit together chewing. He has on his black overcoat, the one he wore to work, but he's wearing jeans and a T-shirt. As nurses walk in and out of the emergency room door, they look at him and smile. A couple of nurses walk back in and out the door a few times. John smiles at each of them, a nice "hello" smile. I wonder what it's like to be him. Ever since I could remember, every girl around him, even younger than me, always stared at him a little longer. Sure, he's handsome, but so is Bobby, so is Martin even. John just has this thing about him, like what movie stars must have—something magnetic.

I give him a one-eyebrow, get-over-it look.

He says, "Big Miss says you're being a divil."

"I'm what?" I can't believe she told him that.

"She says you just walk in and out, don't have anything to do with anyone," he says.

"Really? Does she tell you that I'm in school? Or that I take care of the food shopping and take the laundry?" I truly can't believe how unfair it is that my mother complained to John about me. She lives to be a martyr.

"She's worried about you, that's all. Don't take it so personally," he says.

"How the hell am I supposed to take it?"

"Sorry I mentioned it. Last time I spoke to Momma, I asked her what you were up to, and she told me she wouldn't know," he said. "I'm asking because I want to know what you're up to."

"You can call and ask me," I say.

"You're right, I can, and I will," he says. "But since we're here, fill me in. What's up?"

"It's the same as the last time we talked. School, home, heading out sometimes with a friend, done." *Why am I so hating?* I wonder.

"Did you apply to Brooklyn College or Hunter?" he asks.

I nod, but I'm ready to tell him something that nobody else knows. "Keep this a secret, okay?"

"You got it. What?"

I can't tell if he's anxious to know or just anxious about what the secret is, but he looks like he's bracing for any kind of news. I've told this only to Michael; I don't want to hear everyone's fear or lack of enthusiasm. But suddenly, I truly can't wait to tell John.

"I applied to two out-of-state schools that have serious girls' basketball teams."

His face, right then, is going to make me happy for the rest of my life; I already know that. His smile is ten seconds wide. "Give me five!" he says, both hands out, waiting for the slap.

"One is in Pennsylvania, called Immaculata College, and that's the one Sister Joan, a nun in my school, thinks is a strong possibility," I say. "The other is North Carolina State University, whose women's basketball team is called the Wolfpack. Don't tell anybody!"

"I will not," he says. "Tell me what's the progress of the application. Do you have to go there?" His eyes are boring into me, alert and shiny.

"For Immaculata, I just have to apply and hope for an academic scholarship because they don't have any athletic scholarships yet," I tell him. "They might, in the coming years, but not now. I did pretty good on the SAT, so Sister Joan says they'll be interested in me."

"What'd you get?"

"Twelve hundred. I'm not taking it again, so don't even ask me."

"I wouldn't. That's a really good score."

"North Carolina State actually has some money to give for girls' athletics, but they tend to give it to girls from North Carolina. Sister Joan says if I get an academic scholarship, then I can try out for the team once I'm there."

"When will you find out?"

"By the end of January," I say. "Can you believe it?"

"I believe! I believe!" he says, like he's a preacher. "You have to let me know as soon as you know, Claire. Make sure you have my work number, and call me as soon as you hear anything. What about going there? Do you want to go look at the schools?"

"What for?"

"To see if you like them, genius," he says.

"I already like them. They have great basketball teams."

We both laugh, and I realize I was stupid not to have told John about this when I applied last month. I faked my mother's signature on the financial aid and scholarship form, after stealing a copy of my parents' tax records from their documents drawer. It was a done deal, but John might have helped me write a better essay.

My mother and Martin come out, holding my father's arms between them. John gets up and takes over my mother's side, while she motions for me to join her as she heads out the door. We have to wait in the hallway while Martin goes to get his car, and John goes to get his. It's a little windy out, and my father can't breathe if there's any wind.

We move on the Saturday after Christmas, with a rented U-Haul truck, and Martin's friends doing the hauling. Actually, we do all the hauling. Martin's friends do the heavy lifting. We're done before the morning is over, and we're already carrying things in before the U-Haul gets there. We filled up John's car with clothes, boxes, and small items, then Bobby and I walked over to Sixteenth Street to meet him, where we took the stuff out of the car. You'd think we moved all the time, we're so good at it. But we lived in the apartment on Prospect Park West for almost seven years. It's easy to pack and move when you don't have much stuff.

This apartment has pretty much the same layout as the other one, except it's on the first floor. Walk into a long hall, head out to the first archway where there is a living room, keep heading out to another archway for the bathroom on the right, the kitchen on the left. The bedrooms are at the back end of the hallway, one room with a door, and two rooms separated by an arch. My mother and father get the second room inside the arch, I get the first, and Bobby gets the small room with the door. Just one stop difference on the bus. Hardly a change at all. We live on a street now, instead of an avenue. Same parish.

That Sunday night, the second night we live there, the man

upstairs on the second floor starts beating his wife and two daughters. I know the two girls, slightly, because they are a little younger than I am and go to public school. They never hang around in the schoolyard, and they are always together. The mother is screaming, the girls are crying. The father is cursing, throwing things, slapping them around. He's probably drunk.

I listen for a while and then shake my mother, who is already awake. "Should we do something?" I ask her.

"Pray for them," she says. "That's none of our business, so go back to sleep like a good girl."

I would have woken Bobby up, but he came in bouncing off the walls. The Sunday night Seconal show. God, I hated all of it.

5=OUT MOTION

"**B**aby number two on its way," Martin says, as he is about to leave. He stopped in after work to give my mother some folded-over money. "What do you think, Claire? Want to be the godmother?"

"Yes, definitely!" I say. "When?"

"Probably not until late September, early October," he says.

"God, that's a long way away," I say.

"Maybe your mother should explain to you about how long pregnancy lasts?" Martin is shaking his head, sad for me that I'm a moron.

"You know what I mean, but really, that's so great," I say.

My mother is smiling at Martin, but there's a vertical line between her eyebrows. She can never just take good news; her mind has to find the bad things that could happen. One good thing about the new her: she keeps those thoughts to herself mostly. My father is sitting upright in a chair, looking halfway healthy. My mother is at the beginning of the dinnertime bustle. That's when I see two envelopes on the table for me, propped up against the salt and pepper shakers, like an announcement. Return addresses: Immaculata College, North Carolina State University. My mother must have seen them, but she doesn't say anything. I am too nervous to open the envelopes now, so I grab them, go put them on my bed, and come back to the kitchen.

Martin is not a discussion type of guy. He told us the news; now he's on his way. "How is Genevieve feeling?" my mother asks.

"She's good, no problems, just keeping up with little Jake," Martin says. He's almost out the door as he asks me if I can babysit this weekend.

"Absolutely, I'll be there. What time?"

"Come for dinner. We're going over the Foxes' around eight. Jake should already be asleep," he says.

I'm already thinking I'll ask Michael to babysit with me. He has come over twice when Martin and Genevieve went out. When they came home, they rang the bell, which they never do. I asked Genevieve why she rang the bell, and she told me she didn't. She said Martin did because he didn't want to "walk in on anything."

So they know.

Once Martin is gone, I can't wait any longer. I go to my bedroom, look at the envelopes. They're both thin, which I heard is not a good sign.

Sister Joan asks me all the time if I "heard anything yet." She sees me a lot because her eighth-period math class is right next door to my eighth-period religion class. After she asks me, she always apologizes, as if she's done something terrible. She's like, "Oh, please forgive me, Claire! Of course, you will tell me when you hear anything. I'm so impatient, forgive me."

I always laugh and shake my head at her. She doesn't realize that because she's so anxious, I don't have to be. That's how it works when you're with someone who's nervous.

February 4, 1975. I'm in.

Both letters start off with "Congratulations" and then tell me a packet is on its way. I like that they do it this way. It gives me time to be with "I'm in" and not hurry right away to the details.

I sit on my bed, envelopes in front of me, knowing two things: I have my choice of two "away" colleges, and I'm leaving home.

I know my mother has seen the envelopes, so I should tell her the news, but it's smarter to wait until I know all the angles first, such as how I'm going to pay for it, before I tempt her to dead ball the idea.

I have to figure it out, talk to Sister Joan, talk to John—see how this is going to be accomplished. Not even for four years—let me just see how I can do this for one year. If that works, then I'll plan the second year.

I decide not to think about that and to just spend the rest of the day being psyched. I might even head to the schoolyard to play some ball, though it'll be dark soon. I have two phone calls to make, and one nun to inform tomorrow morning.

I go into my change box, where I have saved nickels, dimes, and quarters left over from every Sunday money since I first started playing basketball. Some weeks, it sees only a nickel from me, others as much as fifty cents. This box of coins won't pay tuition, but that's not what it was ever for. It's for accumulating leftovers. Putting all that's left in one place, adding to it, making it grow. Then using some of it to have a little privacy, a little luxury. I have no idea how much is in this box—it's a little trunk, the size of a big jewelry box. It's not about what the total amount is; it's never going to be enough to pay for those big things like tuition, cars, trips. It's to have a backup in one place for important calls, emergency bus fare, change for the laundromat, an egg cream on a lonely day, buying a secret book of love poetry. Today it's for calls to my brother, then to my boyfriend, to tell them that the "away" colleges said yes. We'll start worrying about how to afford it all tomorrow.

Bobby's hair is almost to his shoulders. He looks like John Lennon, without the glasses. He wishes he was John Lennon, or Mick Jagger. His little room is plastered with album cover posters from *Sticky Fingers*, *Beggars Banquet*, *Sgt. Pepper's*, *Abbey Road*, Led Zeppelin. He's given up taking downers, which is a good thing, even if he is smoking pot and dropping acid like it was candy. Most weekends, he hangs out on the parkside near the monument, where a huge crowd of kids hangs out. Seriously, there must be a hundred of them. They get off the Coney Island Avenue bus at Bartel-Pritchard Square, the last stop, right near the monument. They wear capes and peacoats, headbands and huge bell-bottom jeans. A couple of the girls wear Frye boots, which I am shocked at. How can they afford them? When I visit the games near Washington Square Park, I always walk by this shoe store on Waverly Place that sells Frye boots. I can't believe how much they are. I can't believe girls getting off the Coney Island Avenue bus are wearing them.

Bobby is going out with one of these girls. He is casual about her, and I've never actually met her, but she seems crazy about him. She waits on our corner for him to come out, then walks with him wherever he's going. I said hello to her once; she looked like she was starving or sick. Denise. She's pretty, but she's got too-sad eyes. Something's not completely right about her. I hope Bobby is nice to her.

He has been really nice to me lately—all this year, it feels like. I can't remember the last time he hit me—junior year? It was before we moved to Sixteenth Street. Just, like, one day, Bobby stopped taking it out on me. He works all night cleaning offices, then he goes to Brooklyn College during the day. It's working out good.

"Claire, would you like to go downtown to A&S with me? Maybe we can get you a new outfit?" my mother says, as she comes in through the archway to my bedroom space. I'm reading *Things Fall Apart* for my history and literature AP class. I could use a break.

"When, now?" I ask. It's Saturday morning.

"Yes, I'd like to go before it gets too crowded. Maybe we'll have a bite too," she says.

"Sure, let me get ready," I say. Trips to A&S usually happen right before Christmas and sometimes right after a particularly bad night of drunken rage. This is just a gray March morning. I wonder if she's hoping I'll tell her my college news, but I'm not ready yet.

We walk up to Bartel-Pritchard Square and wait for the Smith Street bus. Even though it's only eleven in the morning, kids are congregating at the monument, dressed in their night outfits. They'll probably be there all day. I look over to see who I know: lots of Bobby's friends, the Coney Island Avenue bus girls, a couple of older guys who went to Woodstock and act like they're still there. A couple of guys hold white cartons of beer from Farrell's Bar & Grill, where Martin drinks after work.

The thing about these kids by the monument, even Bobby, is that I feel like they're in the real world and that I'm not, somehow. I know I look okay, that I fit in. I get looks, whistles, sometimes, but I ignore them. I'm not like them. I don't hang around in groups. I'm more of a lone wolf. That makes me feel weird. Still, I want to shout at everyone on that monument, "What are you doing?" I don't understand, and it makes me sick, that people want to drink, smoke pot, take pills, and hang out all day at the entrance to a park. What for? I would be so lonely if it wasn't for Michael. But even he smokes pot and has drinks with his friends. It's, like, normal. I'm not normal.

My mother and I don't talk on the bus, and she holds her pocketbook as if somebody is going to put a gun to her head any minute.

In A&S, I pick out a light purple skirt with a darker purple striped sweater. It looks good, it'll work for anything—ring day, work interviews, going somewhere nice. My mother charges it, then says, "Let's go to the Garden Room for lunch."

As far as I know, my mother has never, ever, gone to the Garden Room. I for sure have never been. If we get something to eat when we're shopping, we go to Chock full o'Nuts and sit at the counter, splitting a sandwich. I wonder if she can charge the lunch too?

We order our tuna fish on toast sandwiches, and the waitress walks away.

"This is nice, isn't it?" my mother says.

I agree. "Why are we here?"

"I wanted to talk to you, and I thought this would be nice," she says. "You're always so busy, and I wanted to be alone with you."

"What's wrong?"

"Nothing's wrong, for heaven's sake. I'm having lunch with my daughter," she says, but she is too nervous for this place. I better distract her.

"Did you hear Jake read *Goodnight Moon*?" I ask. "He practically knows the whole book. He's so smart for his age."

"He's a whip, that one," she says. "Martin was quick like that, too. You all were . . . Claire, I want to say something to you, and I'm hoping you just listen now and let me finish."

"What's wrong?"

She laughs a little. "Nothing's wrong, I promise you," she says.

The waitress comes with our sandwiches, my mother's coffee, my soda. We thank her; I start to eat. My mother looks at me.

"What?" I say.

"I wanted to tell you—no, I wanted to express something to you," she says. She has practiced what she's about to say, because it comes out like the beginning of a speech. "I want you to know how very sorry I am for the way I behaved when I was drinking."

I put my sandwich down and give her my full attention.

"I was sick," she says. "I did not know how to live my life, and when I drank, I became even sicker. This is not an excuse or even a reason. This is an acknowledgment to you, to *you*, that I have done very bad, very wrong things because of the drink. I have hurt everyone close to me, but I am specifically talking to you, Claire. I am so very sorry for the pain I caused you, and the pain I let happen to you. I can't change that. God knows, I wish to God I could. I am not asking you for forgiveness, my girl. No. I just want you to know that I know in my heart and soul how wrong this was, and I am so very sorry. You are a wonderful girl, Claire. You're so wonderful."

She begins to cry, so she dabs at her mouth and eyes, looks down at her plate, then back at me. I haven't taken my eyes off her. I am horribly, horribly sorry for her. I do not want her to feel this way. I do not need her to tell me how wrong she was or how sick she was. Everything she says, I already know. I know that her behavior was because of the drink—she didn't know that. I know that her rages happened because she didn't know how to be genuinely mad at someone in a normal way—she didn't remember that after her rages. Most of all, I don't want or need her to make some kind of confession to me about how she can look back to see how she was wrong. I knew she was wrong—she knew it too. Even then. She just didn't know what to do about it. So she must have lied to herself about it. Now she knows better because she's not drinking. It's like she's still a little sick, but the cure is not in the drinking. It's in the looking around to see how *she* acts, not how everyone else acts.

"How long has it been since you drank?" I ask. I have an idea, but I want to confirm it.

"Five months," she says. "I stopped drinking on October 17. I haven't had a drink since then."

"So, five months and one week," I say, smiling.

She smiles back. "And one week."

"That's really good," I say. "I'm happy about that, happy for you."

All the way home on the bus, I wonder what I know about actually forgiving someone. Have I ever really forgiven someone? I don't know.

Is forgiveness about understanding? Does it happen automatically, as soon as you think you know why someone behaves the way they do? Do you have a feeling of being neutral, like Switzerland, when you stop being mad at someone, or stop blaming someone for what they've done? Can you forgive someone, if you have a deep-down feeling of disappointment in them? If your soul doesn't feel light around certain people, are you holding them continually responsible for the unhappiness you feel where they are concerned? And the biggest question underneath it all: do I forgive her?

I forgave Bobby, almost immediately, almost every time. No, every time. I've never seen anyone look so sick about themselves, even my mother on terrible hangover days. Bobby's own violence made him sick. Bobby has trouble that he doesn't cause. I see that and understand that, and I truly forgive him because of it. Like, he's *pardoned.*

I am not so sure about my mother. In my heart, I want to forgive her, and I am even willing to. Deep down, the truth is, I don't. I trusted her with my whole heart and soul, with all the love it is possible to feel. Time after time, so many times, she stomped on that. So even though I want to feel forgiveness, I can't bring myself up to that point yet. I blame her. Yes, alcohol made her crazy and hurtful. But she's the one who drank it. Did she say *that* today?

FOURTH QUARTER
APRIL–JULY 1975

COURT VISION

Immaculata College is happening!

In addition to the federal financial aid, they give me five hundred dollars a year, and I'll be working in their cafeteria three days a week for another five hundred dollars. John is already signed up to receive the tuition bills. It's a done deal.

Sister Joan can hardly stand it; I can hardly stand it. Immaculata, the little tiny college in Somewhere, Pennsylvania, just won their third national basketball championship. The Mighty Macs! Nobody ever heard of them here, but they are practically famous in women's college basketball. They play games in huge gymnasiums with gigantic crowds. I wrote about basketball in my essay, but I don't think they accepted me because of that. I haven't even tried out yet. I might not even make the team; it sounds like they're really good.

Since I've been in high school, the rules have changed. They got rid of roving forward and stationary guards. All the players move up and down the court now, just like in men's basketball. Some of the schoolyard play is happening with one-on-one defense instead of zone defense. It's a more aggressive game; everyone has to dribble well, even the guards. The girls in the schoolyard, the younger girls, definitely have to be more on fire. No more standing there waiting for the ball to come back downcourt. There's a lot more hustle to the game and a lot more fouling. Girls are taking it way more personally—thankfully.

Mrs. J., the gym teacher at Bishop who also coaches the intramural basketball games, hates my guts. She used to ref our games at John Jay High School gym when I played for Holy Child. Three years is a long time not to be on a competitive team, and I have to get back in the game. Between now and summer, I plan to play every day. Sister Joan asked and received permission from the dean of students for me to practice in our gym on Tuesdays and Thursdays from three to four thirty. Mrs. J.'s office is right outside the gym. She has a lip snarl when she sees me. I'm not sure she is even aware of it.

"You didn't want to play intramural, so I don't know what you're doing here now," she says, standing outside her door, calling into the basketball court. I'm doing set shots, running for rebounds—basically an adaptation of Kings and Around the World. "You can't make up in two months what you would have gained from being on our team. It was your choice to quit, young lady."

"I know, Mrs. J., thanks," I say, giving her the respectful answer she requires. I don't stop shooting or running. I'm full-body sweating.

"If you think you're going to play basketball for Immaculata, you are going to be disappointed," she says. "Do you have any idea what kind of reputation they have?"

"I know, yes, thanks."

"What about Queens College—you couldn't possibly have tried out for that team. They're actually the best team on the college circuit, a New York City team," she says. "Did they reject you?"

Truthfully, I found out about Queens College basketball only after I applied to Brooklyn and Hunter. It's not like their girls' basketball team was splashed all over the news, or that Mrs. Fitz, the guidance counselor, was any use coming up with the suggestion. Mrs. Fitz, straight-faced, advised me to look at Barbizon School of Modeling because, she said, "You're tall."

"Yes, they rejected me," I say, thinking she'll feel better if she thinks I'm the loser she wants me to be.

"Why didn't you ask me for a recommendation?"

Uh-oh, now she's pissed because she assumes Queens College rejected me. Which, by extension, means they rejected her and Bishop. This, she can't have.

"No, I'm sorry. I mean, I didn't apply there," I say.

She nods, like, "That's more like it."

I'm moving from the center to the basket, dribbling left, right, left, right, shoot layup, dribble back, left, right, left, right.

"Crouch lower," she shouts. "Anybody can steal the ball from the height you're handling it from."

I crouch lower, but I'm getting pretty close to telling her to shove it. Why doesn't she either go in her office or go home? I do my best to ignore her—straighten my face, look intent. I don't trust her. She stands there for a couple of minutes more, just waiting to say something cutting. She's a miserable gym teacher.

She shakes her head, locks her door, and goes down the back staircase. Shithead.

My father walks around with an oxygen tank all the time now. His illness forces my mother to quit smoking. No beer, no cigarettes. My father looks old and frail, like a bag of bones. My mother, on the other hand, looks younger than she ever did. She's rinsing her hair with a dark color Clairol. She's lost that square, bloaty look. When she comes home from her AA meetings, she seems refreshed, like she had some exercise. I don't know if they have the meetings during the day, but she goes every night, right after dinner. She spends a lot of time on the phone, which is completely opposite from what the phone used to signify: a ringer of bad news and emergencies. She treats my father wonderfully, which is a great relief to see. She also babysits for Jake during the day sometimes, so Genevieve can go shopping or to the doctor or whatever she has to do. Most noticeably, my mother doesn't have that look of constant concern, maybe fear, she always had on her face. It's been wiped away.

She sits with John and me in the kitchen, after I tell her about my college plans, quietly listening to him laying out the costs, including his part in them. He tells her he is going to stop giving her the couple of hundred a month he was contributing, and give it to Immaculata and me—plus a hundred more. Money from the federal government will take care of the balance of the tuition, books, room, and board. John is the operations manager now at ADP, so he makes it clear that this is something he can do. I already know I'm going to pay him back every penny.

My mother is fixed on John and doesn't look at me once during this conversation. John shows her on paper how it's going to be perfectly doable. Finally, she speaks.

"What about you?" she asks him. "This is good money that you could be saving. I don't like you doing this."

"I'm going to pay him back," I say.

John smiles, gives me a you're-a-doofus look, and tells my mother, "This works out. I'm making good money. The lease on my apartment is set for the next three years. I'm not anticipating any problem about this. She's going to Immaculata."

I have no question that I am, no matter how reluctant my mother is to part with John's money. John and I high-five. My mother is outvoted.

Michael is going to Boston College in the fall. He's already planning to leave midsummer, a little over two months, to practice for the rugby tryouts. The BC team is highly competitive, and he is completely committed to making it. I admire him. And I really like him. But I don't love him.

I know that because wouldn't I feel torn up by us going to separate colleges? He keeps saying things like, "We'll get together over the weekends," and "Boston is not that far from Philadelphia." I always agree with him, but really, I'm not even thinking it. I sometimes pretend that I'm going to miss him when he talks about how much he's going to miss me.

I've included Michael in my life as much as I can—which is not all that much. I have loved the times we've had, and I love how in shape his body is. He is so nice, still. Maybe I'll love him when I have time later on? For now, I just know that he's been the most special friend I've ever had. The one thing about Michael is, so often, around him, I feel complicated. His life seems so much easier, but I don't just mean his family is rich compared to mine. He's just simpler, somehow. Even though he's on the honor roll at Xavier, and he understands news stories far better than I do, he is exactly what he looks and sounds like. There's nothing hidden.

He's always talking about dreams too: the dreams he has at night, the dreams he is shooting for in the day. I like listening to him; he is so optimistic. He moves from lawyer to stockbroker, doctor to Peace Corps worker, professional rugby player to high school teacher. It's like he's trying these things on, seeing how they fit.

He makes me realize that I've not actually thought beyond college. Like, what do I want to be or do? I don't know. I don't care. I have only ever, and just for the past eight months, focused on the idea of getting there, getting in, getting out of this house, making use of what I'm good at (school, books, basketball). I don't have anything else.

One way of getting out that I thought of way back in second grade was to become a nun. But the only religious vocation I'd want is to be a priest. I'd want to serve Mass and Holy Communion, make my own schedule, wear a cool white collar inside a black shirt. But all religious ideas have been off the table for a long time now, and this year, the requirement of being a virgin is way off the table.

If Michael has a thing that is "bad," it'd be that he likes beer so much. He and his friends get drunk after almost every game. He'll smoke pot too, when his friends have it and the joint gets passed. I've held a joint in my hand, passed it on. I pretend like it's no big deal and that I'll have a toke later, but really I don't need it. I don't want to be a goofball or a head. I'd like to be as far from that as possible—all the way in Malvern, Pennsylvania.

Every Saturday, I'm prepared to sweep and mop the floors of the apartment building. Every Friday night, my mother says, "I did that today, so don't bother." Then she gives me some other chore, like taking the laundry or going to Key Food. I spend Saturday morning doing the family tasks, then go to the schoolyard on Saturday afternoon.

Tina and Diane have been good about meeting me for practice, but they're really not into it. They know I have to get sharp to try out for the team at Immaculata, and they both think I'm lucky for the chance to play college ball, but they're finished with basketball. Tina jogs in Prospect Park; Diane swims at the new Y on Ninth Street. Diane goes to St. Joseph's downtown and is planning to teach kindergarten when she graduates; Tina wants to work on Wall Street as an executive secretary when she graduates high school in June. Still, they both join me in the schoolyard when they can. They want to help.

If I run into Kelly Shea or Shirley, I'll ask them to play too. But even though they were all-stars six years ago, they haven't played basketball since eighth grade. Both of them work full-time in the city now. They used to be great players, and I can't believe they don't miss it, but they say they don't. They also say they are too busy to join me in the schoolyard.

If nobody shows, I play with the younger girls. I don't care, plus these girls are sharp because they're playing every day. They're pretty cool about including me too. I may be four years older than they are, but they have game, and they want to show me. I'm happy for the competition.

The difference between these players now and the girls I played with is that these girls are learning on full-court rules. Every one of them is capable of handling the ball. They're more in-your-face too. In just four years, girls' basketball has left the polite boundaries we had to work with and moved into way more aggressive tactics. The girls in the schoolyard definitely stay with you as you try to dribble past them. They stick with you under the basket. They're all hands out as you jump for the rebound. One of their coaches, Patty Daly, used to play intramurals for St. Edmund. She was a guard who fouled left and right, on purpose it looked like. She's directing these girls to play with a vengeance.

Not our coach—Miss Benedict liked to play smart. She would look over the other team during the first quarter, figuring out each player's weak spot. Then she'd show us plays that would either take advantage of those weaknesses or confound them with surprise. After a while, most players can see what weaknesses or strengths another team has, but taking advantage of it is the coach's job. You need a coach with vision. We were lucky with good coaching.

Basketball is a smart person's game. That's what people don't understand. That's what John taught me: how to see the game from the perspective of using strategy, honing your skills, playing with your head. When I'm in the schoolyard playing, even with these younger, tougher girls, that's the part I realize I miss the most: psyching out the other player, not with trash talk or by being a bully but by figuring out how they're playing their game and strategizing the best way to interrupt it.

Of course, the best strategy is to give the ball to the best shooter. That is, the best shooter should be shooting the most. If I was coaching a team, I would try to make the team be great at three things: getting the ball to the best shooter, knowing when to take the shot yourself, and nailing the foul shot. I would want them all to dribble well, be fast, and all the usual things. But instead of making sure everyone "has a chance," I would play my team with the same strategy as the Knicks: get the ball to the guy who can score; run with the ball as fast as you can, and learn how to take a shot on the run; and dunk that ball in every single time you have the leisure of a foul shot. If you watch the Knicks, they don't really do anything fancier than that. Even Earl the Pearl, with all his magical spinning and shooting, hands off the ball to Walt Frazier all the time because Frazier is the best shooter.

The other most obvious strategy is being great at one-on-one. Stay with your player; breathe like he's breathing; anticipate his next move, and be there before him; and shadow him so hard he can't get free no matter what. This takes so much focus and commitment. It's a winning strategy.

Sometimes, when I think of trying out for the Immaculata team, I get a seizure in my stomach. It's like the Black Power fist is all curled up in there, big as a poster. Thoughts come to me like vicious whispers: *You're not good enough. You've only played CYO. Look how good these younger girls are. You'll get your butt kicked.* And the worst: *Who do you think you are?*

The only solution I have is to dribble the ball, bouncing it harder and harder, lower and lower, until all thinking dissolves in the rhythmic *clutch and push, clutch and push* of dipping the ball.

BASELINE OUT OF BOUNDS

Bobby got an interview with United Parcel Service so he can stop cleaning offices on Wall Street. He'll probably work on the loading dock, he says. Depending on the schedule he gets, he may have to switch to nights at Brooklyn College. Why does everybody think this is a good idea? It will take him longer to finish school. Plus, he'll be working full-time and overtime. But my mother and father are happy, because this is a "good career."

Bobby and I speak usually only in passing. If he has even a hint of high about him, I ignore him completely. If he is straight, he can be a good person to talk to. I just have to remember to wait for him as he catches up to whatever I'm saying. I high-five him, though, about the UPS thing. At least there's a uniform.

John comes over on Sundays to drop money, and his girlfriend stays outside in the car. One afternoon I see her sitting there, so I go over to say hello. Ei-leen. She has dyed blond hair and is wearing a shirt that shows her cleavage. She acts like I'm intruding or doing something rude when I stick my head down to the car window. It's weird. She acts a little guilty too. John comes out on the stoop, waves at me, gives me a hug, then gets in the car. They leave right away— like a getaway.

John smelled like vinegar when he hugged me. He was in such a hurry he barely had the car door shut when it started moving. His hair was still a little wet—from a shower? And he looked like he had a kind of hangover. Like, a drug hangover.

I've gone to the library to read about heroin. It's the worst drug out there and not some big entertainment or party drug. It's addictive. The body will crave it, the medical journal noted, more and more when it's not in the system. John should not be fooling around with this horrible drug.

When I walk into the house, my mother is reading her book. She puts it aside, looks expectantly at me, doesn't say anything. I pace in the kitchen, opening the refrigerator, close it, open it again. My mother says nothing.

Finally, I ask her, "Did you notice anything funny about John?"

"Such as?"

"Such as, he left here in a big hurry, his girlfriend sat in the car outside, he might be taking drugs?"

"That's nonsense. Why do you imagine these things, Claire? John came by here, on his way out for the day, to make good on his promise. Just as he is going to make good on his promise to you. Stop creating stories in your head."

I don't know about her wisdom here. It seems to me that she is way too calm about what happens. This didn't used to be the case. There was a time when my mother would get excited, upset, turn into a basket case about any little thing that happened. Like, when she found out she needed glasses—she cried and screamed in the kitchen like she had cancer. It was ridiculous. And now she's all Buddha when her own son is potentially using the worst drug on the market?

John keeps his business to himself, and my mother doesn't ask any questions.

"So nobody can do anything about this?" I say.

"Claire, I would do anything for any of you," she says. "But I have no power over this, or John, or even you for that matter. It's a sad fact, but it's true. People have to come to their own decisions in life. It's not up to us."

She sounds like she's gearing up to transmit some big philosophy, but I stop her by walking out of the kitchen. "Okay, thanks," I say. I've already decided to call John at work tomorrow and ask him straight out. Tell him what I learned about heroin. Ask him if he is using a needle to take it. Maybe he doesn't know how bad it is.

I call John during lunch period; there is one pay phone near the custodian's office, and I sneak away to use it.

"What's wrong?" he says, as soon as he hears my voice.

"I'm calling because I want to tell you about heroin," I say.

"What the hell?"

"No, listen, I found out that people who use it don't even know they're getting addicted—"

"Whoa, Nellie. Get off this phone right now. I'm at work. Where are you?"

"In school. Lunch. I need you to know that you're crazy to use drugs. And I saw what you looked like yesterday. Your sleeve wasn't rolled down far enough. I saw red marks."

"Hey, you don't get to call me up and start talking like this, you hear me?"

He hangs up. I call him back.

"Can I meet you after work?" I say.

"Are you kidding me? I am working here, Claire. Stop calling right now," he says, beyond aggravated. "I'll see you on Sunday when I stop by. Hang up."

I can't stand not talking to him about this. I head back to the lunchroom planning to go to his apartment tonight. The only problem is he gets home from work at almost midnight.

When I get home, my mother tells me John called, and he'll be at the house on Saturday instead of Sunday. She tells me he said to tell me he's going to shoot some hoops with me.

THE BIG DANCE

"**C**ome on, Little Miss, take the ball. Let's go, move it. What, no, you can't do it, you can't take it, it's not yours. It's my ball, I am the owner of this ball, you can only look at it from where you are. Don't even try it, you can't. You are fouling, fouling, girl. You are losing control, here you go, here you are, can't take it? Going to let me take my shot? Oh no, you do not grab my arm, what kind of bullshit is that, big sorehead, no game. Here I am, here I come, take it away from me, go ahead, Little Miss. Oh no, no, yes, you do, you do. . . ."

I dribble past him to the basket, two points. He laughs.

I am not laughing. He can't make me.

"Little Miss in the corner, dribbling away, so low, wait, the other hand! Oh, now she's faking her way left, now right, can she hold on to the ball? Let's see, oh, she ran past her guard, she's ahead, she's going for the basket! She shoots, scores!"

He is using this singsong announcer voice that is pissing me off. It was funny at first, but he keeps it up, taunting me with it, trying to interrupt my flow. I won't let him. I have the ball, low, crouching, going front, then back, sideways, keeping it low, spinning around away from him, back into the basket, turning around, fake left, go right, sliding past him for the shot: two points.

He is not talking now. His eyes are lit up, alert, ready to play the game with no more fooling around. I am beating him. This is no joke. He runs toward me. I spin one way, then another, head into the basket, stop short pretending to lay up. He jumps up. I wait a hairbreadth second, then jump. Now it's too late for him to get any taste of the ball, and I am free, free, in the air for the shot. It's mine, the sweet spot on the backboard waiting for the quick hit, the ball balanced on the rim, swerving to catch its whirling dance around the edges, tilting ever so ever left, then right, then through. Game.

We sniff, soundless, wordless, breathtaking joy for the ballet, the jazz, the sweet, sweet home of it.

DAGGER SHOT, SIXTH MAN, FLAGRANT FOUL

Sunday morning: my mother is on the telephone, holding on to the wall with one hand, bending over from her waist. "Oh yes, thank you, oh God, oh God, yes, thank you, God bless you. No, you did the right thing, this is good of you. I have to hang up now so I can go to him. Thank you. God bless you." She is talking, crying, praying all at once.

She places the phone gently in the receiver and then drops to her knees on the kitchen floor.

"What is it?" I scream.

She tries to mouth something, but there is only an animal in her throat. She crawls over to me and puts her hands around my legs.

"What is it?" I scream.

She points to the phone. "Call Martin."

I am shaking but make the call. "Martin, Momma needs you to come over right away. It's something bad, I don't know. She can't speak, she's kneeling on the floor!"

I try to pick her up, but she won't budge; she is breathing like she is in a race. My father makes it out to the kitchen from the living room. He has to sit down from the effort.

"Jack, Jack . . ." she cries.

My father kneels on the floor with her, puts his arm around her shoulders. His oxygen tube is crooked. "What is it, Kate, tell me?" he says.

"They found John this morning. He's at Kings County Hospital. In the morgue. We have to go identify him," she says, as if she's reading a newspaper report.

My mother is crazy, wrong, stupid, evil. This is the worst thing she has ever done. I will hate her forever, every single day of my life.

"He was in the bathroom of Louis Garcia's father's house. He must have been there since sometime last night, or early this morning. Mr. Garcia came home and found him. He called the police and the ambulance, but he said he was already dead. He doesn't know where his son is, but he wanted us to know that they took John to Kings County."

My father is crying, and choking because he can't breathe. I sit on the daybed in the living room, staring at my mother on the kitchen floor. I have never hated anyone so much in my life. I think, *if she keeps talking like this, I will murder her.*

Martin bursts in, goes to my mother and father, checking them to see if they are hurt. He is ready to straighten all this out—until my mother starts her disgusting lying all over again.

"Shut *up*! You shut *up*!" I am screaming at her, slamming my feet on the floor, punching the daybed.

I see Martin's face, disfigured, sliding off his head, as he reaches me with both arms stuck straight out like Frankenstein. That's all I know.

All the details come later, too many details. Who wants to know all this shit? It is all shit. It doesn't mean anything. All it means is that John made a final mistake. He thought taking heroin once in a while, on the weekend, was okay. He thought, since he wasn't an addict, and he had a good job and a nice apartment and a girlfriend who liked it too, that he could have his secret drug fun. He could take a needle of this fun and call it a Saturday night.

He didn't know. Forget about becoming addicted. He didn't know how potent this particular batch of heroin was, right? Because if he knew, he wouldn't have taken it. And if Louis Garcia wasn't such a mess himself, if he knew what he was doing, if he wasn't so almost dead from it too, then he wouldn't have run out of his own father's bathroom to leave John there all alone to die. Alone. Right?

Martin and Bobby go to Kings County Hospital to identify the "body." And to arrange for Duffy Funeral Parlor, back in our old neighborhood downtown, to transport the "body" to the place where they will prepare it for burial.

They come back with a plastic bag of John's stuff. Martin is half-drunk; Bobby looks as old as my father. My mother, father, and I sit in the living room, stunned silent. I hold the cold rag that has been on my head. The plastic bag contains his ring, watch, cross, and chain. His clothes. The smell of him.

Martin tells my mother and father that he will bring the funeral parlor a suit, tie, and shirt later today. He will go to John's apartment—he has the keys—and pick out clothes. He starts crying, walks away into the kitchen, opens the refrigerator, slams it shut. He tells us he has to go out now, but he'll be back in a little while. We all know he's going to Farrell's.

My mother wants to know how John looked. She is a devil.

Martin says he looked like himself. He looked "good." Bobby looks at Martin, horrified. Bobby is right to act like that. Why shouldn't my mother know that he looks dead, like a dead man, awful and ghoulish, the way a dead man looks? What does she think? How stupid is she?

My father sits in the chair, breathing oxygen, wiping his eyes and blowing his nose. He has to move the tube around to do that. He and Bobby look so much alike right now. I can see my father in Guadalcanal, then digging the mud to build the Brooklyn-Battery Tunnel, before he married my mother, looking just like Bobby. My father says, "It should have been me," and all of us—me and Bobby, Martin, and my mother—haven't had this thought, but have to admit, somewhere inside ourselves, that it sounds reasonable. We all shake our heads. No.

My mother excuses herself to make a phone call. She is calling the lady, Isabel, who she talks to every day—the lady she reads a book with, the one who helps her not drink. She must be thinking about drinking; why wouldn't she?

John should have known. That's what I'm thinking. Then nobody would have to die for him.

I imagine him on Friday night, making plans with Louis Garcia for Saturday. He must have figured they'd do their drugs, then go out to whatever was next. What was next?

What about his girlfriend? Ei-leen, with her white lipstick, dyed blond hair, and low-cut sweaters? She lived on the other side of Eastern Parkway, almost as far as Queens but still in Brooklyn. They rode around in John's Mustang, but he left her waiting in the car when he came over. Whose idea was that? She liked John, not his family.

And where was Louis Garcia, and why did his father have to call? Why was his father so apologetic to my mother? Why didn't he call our house right away, instead of waiting for the police and the ambulance? Will Martin go to the Garcia house after he spends some time at Farrell's, talking to his cop friends, so he can get some questions answered? What did the official police report say?

There is nobody to ask any of these questions because my family never has answers. John is the only one who answers a direct question.

FIVE-MINUTE OVERTIME
JULY 1975

THERE'S ALWAYS A WINNER IN BASKETBALL

I've been sitting in this church every afternoon for two weeks, just inhaling the smells: faint leftover incense, almost-dead flowers, wood polish. It's like a comfortable funeral parlor without the dead body, just a big wooden crucifix to remind you that a dead body can be had at a moment's notice. On top of all the smells is the papery scent of the host, a parched wafer that softens in your mouth if you suck it or cracks if you bite into it. I haven't had the non-taste of it since John's burial last month. Before that, who knows.

I come here because it feels like a country church, and I imagine that I'm away from Brooklyn—in Connecticut or Vermont, somewhere. I've never been to either. I've been to Upstate New York, but I hate it there. There, it's more depressing than the dirtiest street in Brooklyn, and all the people are misshapen, with fish eyes. I never want to go back there. I'm going somewhere, though. Until then, it's nice coming here on these forever summer afternoons to kill a couple of hours of my life. I can afford it. All the time of my life, it feels like, is in front of me.

That same priest as usual comes in and smiles hello to me. I give him a polite but stiff return smile and turn back to the prop book in my hands. After he passes by, I wonder when it's going to come. When is he going to say enough's enough—what's this girl doing here? He hasn't interrupted me yet, or prodded me for my name, age, grade, or reason why I'm sitting in this church. I have answers ready, just in case. *Doing a silent retreat. Practicing the novena for a spiritual time-out. Reading the Bible in a sacred setting.* A couple of weeks ago, after I first found this church, the priest walked directly toward me, as if he wanted to introduce himself. I have no idea what my face did, but it must have horrified him. His eyebrows spiked up to his scalp, then fell and fluttered into a blank space on his forehead. He kept on walking past me without saying anything. My heart was pounding so bad I swear you could see it move in and out through my shirt.

Now, every day, he comes in after I've been here for about an hour, smiles hello, and goes to the other side of the church, sits down, and prays, I guess. The other side of the church isn't so far away, but it is the other side. After a few minutes, I forget about him. So far he hasn't invaded my time here. I'm betting he won't—unless I start jerking in my pew, foaming at the mouth, and screaming about how much I hate God.

Which is not what I'm doing here. I'm just sitting here because I really need someplace big like a mountain, and there's something about this little church that feels wide and expansive. I'm trying to get my insides to feel like that. What I wish is that I was away from everything, so I could see it all in one view. I wish I could talk to that priest. I'm having a hard enough time talking to myself. Plus, that makes me feel like some old Irish lady who goes to the priest with her troubles and ends up doing fifty Hail Marys and twenty-five Our Fathers: "Now say a truly heartfelt Act of Contrition and go home to fix supper for your family." "Thank you, Father O'Shea, and here's a contribution for the new school."

I don't have anything to confess. I'm eighteen years old. I'm sup-posed to go away in one month to college. I haven't even visited the place yet, and neither has anyone else in my family. Nobody believes I'm really going. Scholarship. Pennsylvania. My mother keeps saying flat-out that I "don't have to go," at least three, four times a day.

One part of my mind knows that she is more afraid than I am.

Another part is busy making up a story so that it will all feel familiar when I get there. I'm trying to push this big hunk of stone out of my heart so I can keep walking toward the person I'm supposed to become. I feel like she's up ahead, already there, waiting for me.

God, I could never say this out loud because out loud, this is crazy. Please don't let me be crazy. So here's my prayer, God: You have to help me. I'm sitting here, every day, suffocating, struggling to breathe around this mountain inside me. It's like the worst pounding headache, only it's in my chest. I keep looking up at your altar, practically begging you to do something. It's exhausting. I've brought myself here every day. Now it's your turn.

This church is nothing like monsignor's church. It's bright, for one thing. One whole side of the church has regular windows, not stained-glass stories darkening the place. The windows on the right side, where I sit, are frosty, but they still allow the trees outside to be seen. It's a small church, like a country church. No kneelers anywhere. Even though it says RC on the sign outside, I've never been in a Catholic church with no kneelers.

In my heart, I'm kneeling. Somehow, I'm praying. *Please help me, God. I miss my brother, and he better be with you. Is he? Please let him be.*

I get on my bike first thing in the morning and ride out to Shore Road all the way from the beginning of Third Avenue—more than a hundred blocks. Third Avenue, after Fifteenth Street, is all cobblestone streets. There's a stretch of ten blocks where empty factory buildings block out the sky to the west, and the elevated BQE blocks the light from the east. In between, only a weak shaft of light manages its way down to the street. Martin told me that all these factories employ people, but since the shipyards closed down, and the factories have no reflective windows, the whole area looks empty. It could be a movie set, with only the fake facades and nothing behind them. This is Bush Terminal, where block after block, from Thirtieth to Fortieth Street, massive, six-story, dirty-gray buildings loom. By Forty-Third

Street, the Lutheran Medical Center takes over. The only thing to watch for here is the cabs and car services dropping people off. This area is mostly Puerto Rican, and the people getting out of the cabs seem like parents whose kids need to go to the emergency room. They use the emergency room as their regular doctor. So does my family.

By the time I get to Shore Road, everything changes. From the broken-down, empty look of Third Avenue, an underpass signals the end of the neighborhood. On the other side of the underpass is Bay Ridge and Shore Road. Here the streets are paved, marked by neat yellow lines in the middle. The sky opens up; the Hudson River becomes the personal view of the people who live in the luxury buildings that curve along the thirty-block length of Shore Road. After Seventieth Street, this view is bracketed by the sky sculpture of the Verrazzano-Narrows Bridge.

The Verrazzano bridge is one word: beautiful. If it's early enough in the morning, the blue steel looks cold and new. In the afternoon, if it's really hot, it shimmers like a mirage. The sky looks like it is melting around it, as clouds break apart around its arches. If I stare at the bridge long enough, and I always do, I imagine I can see it sway. Just seeing the arches brings the whole world smack into my brain. Like Martin said, they made the towers farther apart at the top because they had to take into account the Earth's curvature. They had to plan around the Earth.

I have to plan around myself. My head is fuzzy, and I don't know myself.

This morning is completely still, hardly a breeze, even by the bridge. By the afternoon, it'll be murderous. I look like I ran through an open hydrant after riding out here. There's nobody out at all, even by the water, by the bridge. I sit on a bench overlooking the bay and the bridge. I have no thoughts.

On the way to the church, I walk my bike by the handlebars, lifting my elbows up to air out my underarms.

The church is incredibly cool. I sit in my usual row, already beginning to feel sleepy, like I'm in a kind of sanctuary. The Host is on reverent display in the monstrance on the altar. The sunburst gold receptacle winks in the light, sitting on a white tablecloth. Behind it, the smooth wood of the wall cross seems to bow toward it. I see a fleeting image, a ghost, of John wearing that fake cross at the band shell. Is today a holy day of obligation? No, it's still July, no holy days. Nobody's here yet, so whenever the people come to adore the Host, I'll slip out.

O my God, I am heartily sorry for having offended thee. And I detest all my sins because I dread the loss of heaven and the pains of hell.

The Act of Contrition—the "I'm sorry" prayer. Memorize it. Repeat it to the priest in the confessional, so you can be absolved of sin and receive the Body of Christ. Go behind the heavy velvet drape, tell the priest what you did wrong—disobeyed four times? Lied two times? Hated somebody?—and wrap it up with this prayer. Because just saying "I'm sorry, God" isn't good enough. You have to back it up with words like "heartily" and "detest." And get on your knees. Money in the bank for when you die. Sunday Mass, the formal visit, where attendance is taken.

I'm sorry for *you*, God. I'm mad at you, and that's all there is to it. You art all deserving of all my loathing. I'll say the Act of Contrition, and I'll talk in my head to you about how I really feel. I'm coming here every day, but when I leave church this afternoon, I might not come back tomorrow.

Remember our most precious Virgin Mary, that ever was it known, that anyone who fled to thy protection, implored thy help, or sought thy intercession, was left unaided. Inspired by this confidence, we fly unto thee, O Virgin of virgins, our Mother. To thee I come, before thee I stand, sinful and sorrowful. O Mother of the Word Incarnate, despise not our petitions, but in thy mercy, hear and answer them. Amen.

My mother and father are paying for the balance of tuition at Immaculata. They insisted, they implored, they beseeched. For John. My mother showed me an account she had in the bank, like a Christmas club. She's been putting money away—sometimes five dollars a week!—for years and years. It's a little maroon passbook with a rubber band around it; she keeps it in an old pocketbook of hers in the back closet. That's how they had enough money for the funeral and the cemetery plot. That's how she'll be able to pay the balance of my tuition, at least for this year.

The priest comes in, goes to his side of the church. I'm used to him by now. I expect him to be here. Today, though, he stops by my pew. He made it very clear that he was on his way to where I'm sitting—coughing, waving, smiling his way over.

"I haven't introduced myself to you, and I want to apologize for that," he says. He's young, Irish looking, clean-faced. "My name is Father Danny Murphy, and I'm so very happy to meet you."

I shake his hand, smile on one side of my mouth. "I'm Claire." I start the automatic scanning—sensing for signs of phony, threat, mental, idiot. None. The channel is open, alert to any signs that this priest if off in any way. If he is, I'll know it. My alarm system usually doesn't fail.

"Claire, you know, I want you to know that I am the pastor of St. Andrew's, and I don't know if you know this, but we have quite a thriving community here. There are prayer groups, and there's a teen night on Friday nights. We also organize trips to places like Jones Beach. We just had our Fourth of July picnic, but I don't think you were coming here then. No matter, I just wanted you to know that, of course, of course, I am delighted that you make use of the solitude during the weekdays—isn't it wonderful to have this?—I know how much it soothes my soul to be able to come here to pray, or read, or even just to be quiet. And I hope you continue to come, please. Okay, now I'm talking way too much about how much I love the solitude, and here I am, interrupting yours—"

"No, it's okay." I was kind of laughing because when he said he was talking way too much, he rolled his eyes and nodded as if he knew what he was doing was stupid, and that he thought it was stupid, but he was doing it because he couldn't help it, because he was stupid. Father Danny is definitely honest; he means what he is saying. He isn't just talking. He has left me alone for two straight weeks. Now he's doing his best, dancing as fast as he can, to say, "I'm here, but I'll go away, but I'm here, so use me if you want to, or I'll get out of your hair, but don't worry, I won't haunt you, I'll just be around . . ." His struggle—was it nervousness?—makes me feel calm. I like that about him.

"Father, I really do like it in here," I say.

"Oh, thank you, Claire, you're very kind. But look, I'm going to leave you alone, but I want to invite you to come to Mass here on Sunday, this Sunday, because we're having a breakfast afterward downstairs in the parish room. Did you know we have a big room downstairs? Now I'm just talking too much, so I'll say good after-noon to you, Claire. I'm so happy to see you here. God bless you."

As he turns to go, I open my mouth, as if I'm going to say some-thing. Nothing comes out. He walks a few steps, then turns around, giving me a full-faced, unfaked look. His eyes are what gets me. This priest, this Father Danny, has eyes that know a God who I haven't met. His eyes are pale and frank, wide open, knowing something but keeping quiet about it. I feel my head tilt in his direction. With a quick blessing, Father Danny gently flicks north and south, west and east, before walking away.

I suddenly realize that I've been sitting here, hoping something will happen to me. I don't know how I'm going to get where I'm going.

But the real failure would be to not even try. Someone has had faith in me since I can remember. Someone is beside me, always.

I compose myself, ready to take the long ride home.

ACKNOWLEDGMENTS

Gratitude is so joyful. With full heart, thank you to:

She Writes Press for saying yes. Brooke Warner, for her greenlight philosophy. The designers who captured the novel's spirit; Addison Gallegos for her gracious stewardship.

The incredibly generous writers, editors, agents I was lucky enough to learn from at various junctures on this journey. What wonderful people. Personal thanks coming their way.

Other writers, forever: My Third Monday writer's group. RockWriters. Living Room Workshop. The many circles I've sat and read and been bowled over in…so much talent out there.

Residencies who invited me (more than once!) to come there and write, especially Yaddo and Ragdale.

Literary Magazines, who made the last year so encouraging: Cleaver, Embark, Lakeshore Review, among them.

Friends who always kept *this* light on for me – Liz Palombo, Lizi Moses, Emily Grandinetti, Bonnie Daly, Theresa McCann, Lisa Sardinas.

Spiritual warriors who arm me with prayer and power. Your names are etched on my heart.

My sons, my sons: Luke Hill. Adam Hill. Oh man. What love.

Howard Hill – the beating heart of it.

Next generation: Madison Hill, for the wonderful things you will be.

ABOUT THE AUTHOR

photo credit: Hancock Headshots

Maggie Hill's essays and non-fiction pieces have been published in The New York Times, The New York Daily News, and Scholastic professional magazines. Current publications include Lakeshore Literary Review, Cleaver Lit Mag, Embark Literary, and Persimmon Tree. She has been the recipient of several artist fellowships and residences, including Yaddo and Ragdale. *Sunday Money* is her first novel. www.MaggieHill.com

SELECTED TITLES FROM SHE WRITES PRESS

She Writes Press is an independent publishing company founded to serve women writers everywhere. Visit us at www.shewritespress.com.

I Like You Like This by Heather Cumiskey. $16.95, 978-1-63152-292-5
In 1984 Connecticut, sixteen-year-old Hannah Zandana—cursed with wild hair, a bad complexion, and emotionally unavailable parents—is miserable at home and at school. But when she gets the attention of Deacon, her high school's handsome resident drug dealer, her life takes an unexpected detour into a dangerous and seductive world.

I Love You Like That by Heather Cumiskey. 16.95, 978-1-63152-616-9
In this sequel to *I Like You Like This*, Hannah—reeling from the loss of Deacon, her dark and mysterious former boyfriend and first love—lets herself fall into the arms of the wrong boys, even as her mother's growing addiction continues to pull her family apart.

Keep Her by Leora Krygier. $16.95, 978-1-63152-143-0
When a water main bursts in rain-starved Los Angeles, seventeen-year-old artist Maddie and filmmaker Aiden's worlds collide in a whirlpool of love and loss. Is it meant to be?

Shrug by Lisa Braver Moss. $16.95, 978-1-63152-638-1
In 1960s Berkeley, teenager Martha Goldenthal just wants to do well in school and have a normal life. But her home life is a cauldron of kooky ideas, impossible demands, and explosive physical violence—and there's chaos on the streets. When family circumstances change and Martha winds up in her father's care, she must stand up to him, or forgo college.

Stitching a Life: An Immigration Story by Mary Helen Fein
$16.95, 978-1-63152-677-0
After sixteen-year-old Helen, a Jewish girl from Russia, comes alone across the Atlantic to the Lower East Side of New York in the year 1900, she devotes herself to bringing the rest of her family to safety and opportunity in the new world—and finds love along the way.